Hot! In Tomales

A Detective Mark Johnson Mystery

Also By John C. LaBella:

<u>THE SECRET OF THE FARALLONES</u>
A Detective Mark Johnson Mystery

<u>THE INSIDE OF OUTSOURCING:</u>
A Pragmatic View From The Inside

<u>WINNING IN THE WORKPLACE</u>

Hot! In Tomales

A Detective Mark Johnson Mystery

John C. LaBella

Published in the United States by LCI,
an imprint of LCI Publishing Group.
Madison, Wisconsin.

ISBN: 978-0985553661
Printed in the United States of America MMXVIII.

Cover design and graphics by:
Kurt B. Schoenfielder, Throttle 5 Design
www.Throttle5.com

Technical and fire fighting protocol by:
Chief George L. Burke, MFD Retired

Inspiration from my forever partner:
Patti LaBella

Disclaimer:
This is a work of fiction. Although it references actual
historical events, all names, characters, places and
incidents are a product of the author's imagination.
Resemblance to actual persons, living or dead,
businesses, events, or locales is entirely coincidental.

Dedicated to the memory of two people who made a difference in my life...

Rosalia LaBella, my mother, an avid Green Bay Packers fan, who enjoyed watching Aaron Rodgers on and off the field. She was 100 years old when she left this world in November 2017.

Joe Van Tuyle, my father-in-law, a lifelong Chicago Cubs fan, who lived long enough to see the Cubs finally win the 2016 World Series. Joe was 91 years old when he left us in December 2017.

Chapter 1

The roar of raging fire, shattered glass crashing to the floor, and doors slamming shut had awakened her from a deep, peaceful sleep. She lie there, alone, paralyzed with fear, unable to move. *Had someone broken in?* Pulse racing and heart pounding, nearly exploding out of her chest, she turned a glance to the clock an arms length away on the nightstand. *One minute after two o'clock in the morning.* A table lamp and a pair of reading glasses sat next to the clock. There was also a telephone and a bottle of Tums, used to ease the constant heartburn from the litany of medications she took.

Walking briskly from her house, an unnoticed stranger moved along side streets, quietly melting into the mist. A light fog, the type that cuts through your bones, was moving in from the bay. A cold looking haze, a halo of sorts, had formed around the full December moon. Some say that ice crystals in the atmosphere are the cause of it – others called it the Witching Moon. In this desolate part of Western Marin County, feelings of seclusion, peace, and even aloneness affect, or may actually attract, those with the resilience to call it home.

Cool breezes pick up when seasons move from fall into winter. Bare of foliage, trees stood naked in the fading moonlight. Pushed by an occasional gust, crisp autumn leaves, red, yellow and orange, danced through the vacant streets of Tomales, California. Some found their way through the wrought iron fencing that surrounds the cemetery. That fence had long stood guard over the dead buried behind the old Presbyterian Church. Graves, above ground due to the solid granite sub-surface, had become the final resting place for leaves too.

Most of the people in this town were fast asleep...but not all. Smoke began flooding her senses. Something was wrong. Within seconds a hellfire was raging down the hall a few feet away. She reached for the phone to call 9-1-1. "Hello? Hello? Damn it." Numbers on the clock, illuminated just seconds earlier were now dark. She realized that her phone was dead. No power. Frantic.

At two minutes after two o'clock in the morning she managed to get out of bed to find the front room of her modest one-story house fully engulfed in flames, an inferno. The conflagration quickly climbed the flowered draperies and reached the ceiling. Searing hot combustion, a canopy of fire, quickly overspread the room. HOT. Breathing became difficult. With no way to get to the front door she realized that her only chance for escape from this, her personal hell, was through the kitchen and out the back door of the house.

She found it difficult to catch a full breath and gasped for air. At three minutes after two o'clock in the morning the entire house was filled with thick, noxious smoke – black smoke. HOT smoke.

Her knees buckled. She fell to the floor, hard, but was determined to make her way to the rear door. Using every last ounce of strength she fought to get outside – to the COOL, to freedom, to life.

Suddenly, flames flashed overhead, strafed by the fireball erupting in front of her she faced another explosion of fire and heat. HOT. Heat was pressing down on her. At four minutes after two o'clock in the morning, flames dripped from above onto her polyester nightgown as she finally, in one last push, reached the door.

Gotta' get out. The doorknob turned in her hand when she grabbed it, but the door was jammed. She could not open it. HOT. Flesh from her palm seared onto the knob. She crumpled and fell to the floor one last time, just inside the door.

Intense heat melted her nightgown, pieces of it stuck to her skin. Burning debris from the ceiling rained down, partially covering her. Singed by the flames, her silver hair was mostly gone; a few lone strands remained. The searing pain replaced the beauty in her face with a grimace. Her skin became taut from ever-present heat. HOT. Escape denied. Fire had claimed one more life. Grace Loomis breathed her last at five minutes after two o'clock in the morning.

Just two blocks away stood a Marin County fire station on Dillon Beach Road. The fire crew arrived in minutes. By then the flames had fully consumed the wood-frame house. Neighbors, eleven or twelve of them, had assembled to watch from across the street. Concerned about why another home in Tomales had burned, someone in the crowd yelled, "Looks like it's a 'torch job'..." Another cried out, "There's an arsonist at work here." The people of Tomales were scared. Three fires had occurred within the span of a few weeks.

Hidden within the shadows of the crowd, a curious on-looker watched intently as the flames consumed the structure. A navy blue hoodie was pulled tight, hiding the face. Black pants and dark gloves covered the rest of the onlooker, making it impossible to tell if this person was a man or a woman. Rubber boots, wet from the evening dew, seemed out of place with the rest of the ensemble. *When will they bring out the body? I need to make sure the old bitch is dead.*

* * *

"Hello...?" said a groggy voice.

"You better get your butt up to Tomales," said Billy Dibdall. "Dispatch just called. There's another one burning." Dibdall, Marin County Fire Marshal was calling from the Fire Service Headquarters in Woodacre, California.

"Sure thing, Cap. I'll...ah...I'll be there in thirty minutes or so."

"Who is calling you at this hour?" Jenny asked in a quiet voice, as she lay with him, warm and cozy under the covers.

With his left hand covering the mouthpiece, he turned to her, "Shhh – would you please be quiet? It's Dibdall." Speaking into the phone he said, "This is the third fire in as many weeks. Gotta' be arson, Cap. I want to get on scene before the hose jockeys wash away all the evidence."

Half asleep and three quarters drunk, Jerzy Grotowski was anxious to get to Tomales, eager to investigate this fire. Jerzy was his birth name, which translates to George in Polish. When he was young, his family had given him the nickname of 'Jurek,' a name that stuck with him.

"Are you ok to drive, Jurek?" asked Dibdall.

"Hey baby, do you have to go?" asked Jenny in a soft voice. "I don't want to stay here all alone."

Jurek was trying to manage two conversations at once. "Hold on," he mouthed to Jenny, putting his finger over her lips. "Yeah, sure, Cap," said Jurek. "We tipped a few in honor of Jack. You knew about Jack Parker's retirement party last night, right? The guys toasted him at The Mayflower bar." When a firefighter retires, it's a big deal, a right of passage always celebrated heartily.

"Jack was my mentor when I first joined up," said Dibdall. "Thirty years of service? Wow, sorry I missed that one. By the way, Jurek, who did you take home this time?" Dibdall knew that Jurek and his long-time girlfriend, Jenny, had a bad break-up a few months earlier. He also knew that Jurek did not have a problem meeting the ladies, but no one could ever take the place of his Jenny. Dibdall had no idea that Jurek and Jenny were together again – at least for the night.

"Cap, I had a couple of beers and was home by midnight – by myself. The only people at the party were firefighters and none of them are my type."

"It's not nice to lie," Jenny whispered into his ear. The tip of her tongue flitted erotically along his cheekbone. "We were both pretty buzzed up when we staggered in and it was closer to one am."

Jurek took the phone and placed his large hand firmly over the mouthpiece so Dibdall wouldn't hear him. "Jenny, I know. I was planning to sleep in and finish up some stuff around the house. Now I've got to get out to the scene and manage another investigation. Someone's killing with fire."

"Okay, Jurek," she said, propping herself up on her forearm. She made sure her gorgeous curves were in plain view, hoping to entice Jurek into staying. Finally she said, "Go do what you have to do. I understand. Just be damn sure you come back and put out the fire *we* started."

Still on the phone, Dibdall said to him, "Get up and get dressed. Call me from the car once you're in route and I'll fill you in on the details."

Jurek got out of bed, stretched to loosen up the muscles in his back and legs and threw some clothes on – the same clothes he had worn to the party. They smelled of bar smoke, but he was going to a fire for Christ's sake, not a style show. What did it matter what he looked like or smelled like. He didn't waste time brushing his teeth either. He would clean up when he came home later. A Blade-Tech holster, with his 9mm pistol in it, sat on the nightstand next to his bed. Jurek snapped the holster onto his belt and checked to make sure the magazine was in place. He was out the door and in his pickup five minutes after getting the call from Captain Dibdall.

* * *

This was the third fire in Tomales, California in the past few weeks. Jurek was determined to get to the scene before the firefighting crew had destroyed the evidence with an aggressive overhaul. After the initial fire has been knocked down, the crew will overhaul the scene looking for small fires or rekindles to make sure it is completely out. As Jurek drove to the scene he called Dibdall. "Cap, I'm in route. Did you ever do the math on the random chance of three fires being set this close together?"

"No, I haven't. I don't know what the number is but I would guess the chances are pretty small."

"Right, Cap. Tomales is a small town of about two hundred people. Three structure fires in five weeks? It's more than coincidence – it's gotta' be the work of an arsonist."

"I agree, but there wasn't any evidence of arson found in either of the first two fires."

"Was the death in the first fire ruled accidental?

"Yes, it was."

"Who was the investigator?"

"Sam Rollins."

"You mean, DBI? Rollins is the original 'Drive-By-Investigator'."

"Jurek, Sam's been around a long time. Can't you try to show just a little respect?"

"Cap, I respect his years of service but he's just not a thorough investigator. A dead bull could drop from the rafters and Rollins would miss it."

"Say, Jurek. Since you'll be in Tomales, I would like you to do a follow-up on the first fire too."

"Sure. Maybe we'll get lucky and the evidence we need will still be there, hopefully intact."

"Jurek, do you recall learning that every fire has a unique personality?"

"Yes, Cap. I do."

"Plus, those fire science classes you took taught you that fires are predictable. They always follow a pattern." Dibdall knew Jurek was exhausted and was trying to keep him awake by talking to him. "You learned arsonists are a pretty stupid lot. They leave evidence behind, thinking the fire will destroy it."

"Yeah, yeah, yeah. What's your point, Cap?"

"My point, Smartass, is that cases are solved when an investigator combines fire science with the stupidity of the arsonist."

"Yeah, right out of the academy, Cap. 'Fire Investigation 101'; fires have a specific origin and they always follow a path."

"Right, Jurek."

"You taught that class, Cap."

"And you learned it better than any of the other students." Dibdall agreed with Jurek that each of the first two fires was the result of arson. It was a feeling in his gut but he needed evidence in order to convince the county supervisor that this was the work of a serial arsonist. Being declared "serial" is an important distinction, one that would warrant some additional resources from the Marin County Sheriff's Office. Without those resources, Dibdall's unit would have to manage the investigation and ultimate arrest of the arsonist on their own. This would put a tremendous strain on a limited number of resources in the fire investigation unit. "Jurek, I'm counting on you to get to the scene and find the evidence we need to expand the case. Drive carefully."

Chapter 2

Thirty miles separates the tiny town of Tomales, California from Jurek's apartment. The curvy drive along Highway 1 follows the contours of foothill canyons leading to Tomales Bay. A difficult road to drive in broad daylight with its many switchbacks and tight turns, at night with heavy fog it was near impossible to see the pavement. Wisps of fog, pushed up from the Pacific Ocean, climbed the canyon walls and blanketed the highway. Jurek had grown up in the area and learned to drive on these roads. The steep drop-offs that plummet into deep ravines did not rattle him. He would be fine as long as he could manage to stay on the road.

Suddenly, the inside of the windshield on Jurek's pick-up started fogging up, a common event when driving through a cold air bank. The glass is super chilled on the outside, allowing warm moist air inside the vehicle to condense on the glass. A mistake, made by many drivers, is to turn on the defroster thinking that warm air will clear off the windshield. Jurek, experienced driving in fog, did the opposite. He turned the defroster fan to high then he set the AC to max. Within seconds the windshield cleared. After what seemed like hours, Jurek saw the flashing lights of emergency vehicles reflecting off the low hanging fog bank, creating an eerie glow. He knew he was close.

The firefighters had finished knocking down the flames moments before Jurek arrived. Arsonists are egocentric and enjoy watching their work. The first thing Jurek does is to photograph the crowd of on-lookers that always assemble to watch the fire. He would study the pictures closely later.

Jurek always followed protocol. He went up to a young firefighter and asked, "Where's the officer in charge?" The young man was exhausted. His gear, covered in heavy black soot, would need to off-gas, or air out, when he returned to the station.

"Lieutenant Craemer is the OIC, sir," the young man replied. "He's over there." Before Jurek would enter the structure he would make an effort to find Craemer and introduce himself.

"Glad to see the cops are here," Craemer said in a snide way. Jurek was, in fact, a cop. Marin County grants that fire investigators have full Police Powers. This means that solving arson-set fires must follow specific rules of criminal investigation, especially as it pertains to collecting evidence and questioning suspects. Fire investigators are also authorized to carry firearms. Jurek had to complete additional training in police protocol, well beyond that of basic fire investigation. This training prepared him to not only carry a weapon, but to question suspects as well. He also learned how to work cooperatively *across* the various agencies within law enforcement.

Jurek ignored Craemer's comments. He knew it would quickly escalate into an argument. Craemer was "old-school" and had a bad reputation with other investigators. "What have we got Lieutenant?" asked Jurek.

"It's another single story shit-shanty in beautiful Tomales, California. It's old, weathered and the siding has dried out. The structure is falling apart."

"Right, Lieutenant. Any idea as to how the fire started?" asked Jurek.

"Who the hell knows? The roof is covered with oil soaked tarpaper. It's the perfect tinderbox for any spark that might happen to come along. Your job is to figure out where that spark came from."

"How soon can I get in to look around?"

"We're done knocking down the flames so feel free to gear up and take a look. Oh, the guys found the remains of an old lady near the back door."

Jurek had arrived in time to walk the scene while most of the evidence was still in tact. Standard procedure for the crew is to cut off electric service. Still dark outside, Jurek grabbed a flashlight from his glove box and walked to the back of his truck to put on his turnout gear and breathing unit.

A fire investigation kit is always at the ready in his truck too. The kit included empty metal paint cans, with lids. He had two one-gallon cans and each had a one-quart and a one-pint can nested inside of it. One of the cans would be used to collect an evidence sample and the other would be used to collect a control sample.

"Make sure you put those pants on straight," yelled Craemer, as Jurek put his gear on. "The fly goes in front. Or maybe in your case, Nancy, it's on the side." Jurek stepped into his boots, and hiked up his pants, followed by his flame retardant jacket and helmet. The last thing he put on was his Self Contained Breathing Apparatus (SCBA), which was stored in a locked box in the back of his truck. Jurek was ready. Moments after entering the building, the face-piece on his breathing apparatus, chilled from sitting in the back of his truck, began to fog up. The water used to fight the fire had created a humid environment in the structure. Even though it was contrary to procedure, Jurek removed his face-piece.

Hot! In Tomales

Almost instantly three smells flooded his senses:

1. Kerosene – Jurek determined that it was the accelerant used to push the fire. It has a distinct smell and it is widely available. Local ranchers use it to heat their homes and barns.

2. Burnt fabric – from the drapes and furniture.

3. Rancid garbage in kitchen – it smelled of fish.

Timbers had fallen from the rafters with pieces of the ceiling still connected to them. As he moved towards the rear of the structure he could see that the building was a total loss, nothing to salvage. Finally he detected a fourth smell – the acrid stench of burnt hair and flesh. It gagged him every time. The odor was strong, which told him he was getting close to the victim's body.

The beam from Jurek's flashlight reflected off something near the door. There, lying in a pugilistic state were the remains of a person. The intense heat causes muscles to contract and the arms will often curl up into a boxing position, close to the chest, leaving the person looking like a prizefighter.

The body was difficult to see. Pieces of charred drapery had fallen down on it. Jurek would have missed it if his light had not landed on a shoulder. As he looked closer, he saw a charred upper torso; it was the body of a female. Her face, with its torrid smile, was staring at him – no, it was staring through him. He lifted away some debris with his hand to find that her clothing had mostly been burned away. Her charred skin exposed. The few wisps of silver hair told Jurek that she was an older woman. Fire victims are awful sights and Jurek had never gotten used to finding them. It was gag time and he needed some fresh air – right now.

Jurek retraced his steps back through the house being careful not to disturb any evidence. Always scanning the scene for clues, Jurek noted that the top of the couch was badly burned but the floor underneath appeared to be untouched by the flames. As he walked past the dining room table he noticed two saucers. Strangely, one still had a teacup on it. *How in the hell did that teacup escape the force of the water hose?* A larger plate and a fork had crashed to floor near the table. Scattered around the plate were eighteen or twenty oysters, an oyster knife used to pry them open and a few charred lemon wedges. *Was her last meal oysters?*

Finally he reached the front door and noticed the old fashioned lock on it. A skeleton key, the kind sold at any hardware store, was left in the entry side. Jurek stepped outside. The refreshing night air was a relief for him. Jurek sketched the scene while it was still fresh in his mind. He knew the woman's death was murder and vowed to get her justice.

16

Hot! In Tomales

After extinguishing a fire, standard procedure calls for the crew to re-enter and overhaul the scene. Water is used to flush out hotspots and eliminate re-kindles. As the crew prepared to go in Jurek yelled out. "Hold up a minute, guys. I'm not done in there yet. I need another thirty minutes to finish before you hose away what's left of the evidence. The victim's body is still in there and I need time to figure out *how* and hopefully *why* she's dead."

"Hold up guys," Craemer told his men. Turning to Jurek he said, "You got twenty minutes. We have to button things up, get the rig back to the station and make it available for service. The next crew is arriving at seven. Oh yeah, and put your mask on, rooky. CO_2 readings are still too high."

"Neanderthal hose jockeys," Jurek was heard muttering under his breath as Craemer walked away, not intending to insult Neanderthals. It's true that Jurek was younger than most firefighters in Marin County. He had eight years of service but in no way was he a "rooky." Unfortunately, Craemer refused to cut him any slack.

"I ain't gonna' be givin' mouth-to-mouth to a dumb cop. Put that mask on," yelled Craemer.

Jurek looked at his watch. He knew he had to get back in and be done by five fifteen. He put the mask on, more for show than anything else, and re-entered the building. The face-piece on his SCBA fogged up just like it had before. When he was out of Lt. Craemer's sight, Jurek pulled it off again.

Jurek methodically worked his way back to the woman's remains, looking for other victims and, of course, additional evidence. Fortunately, he found no other bodies. Stopping to take a closer look at the bathroom, he did notice a number of medicine bottles sitting on a glass shelf under the mirror over the sink. Although the heat had partially melted them, he knew the lab could get useful information from them. He tagged them for the forensics team to take for examination.

Jurek continued to the rear of the building and found what appeared to be charred flesh on the rear doorknob. *Did the flesh come from the victim?* He missed it the first time and tagged this piece of evidence for the forensics team to examine. Maybe they could lift prints from it or at the very least, match the DNA to the deceased woman. This was an important find. If it were the victim's tissue it could prove that she died trying to escape the fire through the back door. If he proved the fire was set intentionally it would be murder by arson.

Suddenly a chill ran down Jurek's spine. He was looking at something that convinced him that this was not an accidental death.

Chapter 3

"Hey, Cap. It's Jurek. I can't believe it, I found a trailer." Jurek had called Dibdall's phone, anxious to tell him about his find. Skilled arsonists are capable of using trailers to direct the path of a fire. A small amount of accelerant is applied to the floor that connects two target areas. Shortly after the initial fire is raging, the accelerant on a "burn trailer" will flash over, quickly pushing the fire to the secondary ignition point.

"I heard that an old woman died in the fire. Tell me what you found, Jurek."

"I'd say the victim was in her seventies and died from extensive exposure to the heat. She was pretty crisp and all curled up when I found her."

"Was an accelerant present, Jurek?"

"I noticed a strong kerosene smell and found two, two-quart kerosene containers; one in the front room and the other in the kitchen."

"Four quarts? That's a lot of kerosene."

"I know. Patterns in each of the rooms tell me that there was a major ignition in each. I'll scrape up residuals from the initial and the secondary ignition points for testing in the lab."

"*Initial* ignition? Where did you find each of the containers again?"

"I told you, one was in the front room used to set the initial fire. The other was used to create the burn trailer from the front of the house to the rear, which is where the second stage of the fire started. I believe the kerosene can I found in the kitchen was poured on the hallway floor to make the trailer. I'll collect samples from the trailers too." Shortly after Jurek had been hired, Dibdall recognized his interest and aptitude for fire investigation. Jurek studied hard and became Fire Investigator about five years ago.

"I'm glad to see all of that training is paying off, Jurek." Dibdall had seen something special in Jurek and convinced the county to invest in his training. Jurek had recently returned from his third trip to the National Fire Academy in Emmitsburg, Maryland. Each time Jurek attended a training class he learned something new that would increase his knowledge of fire investigation and police protocol. He was a good student and had recently passed his National exams to become a Certified Fire Investigator.

Hot! In Tomales

"Once any fall down debris is removed, a burn trailer sticks out like a sore thumb, if you know what to look for. This one runs from the front room to the kitchen in the rear. There are distinct marks and blisters on the linoleum floor, Cap."

"I thought you were talking about the burn trail that set off the initial fire. A secondary ignition is rare and the timing is hard to control. The son-of-bitch that set this fire ain't no rooky, Jurek. Watch yourself." Accelerant trailers are difficult to stage, especially in occupied structures. In this case, the first fire started in the front room and the secondary fire in the kitchen. "In order for this to be done, the arsonist must have been in the structure right before the fire started in order to set up the trailer and then start the initial fire. Any sign of forced entry?"

"He used a skeleton key to get in."

"What?"

"The front door has a skeleton lock on it."

"What else?"

"I've chalk-marked the area for forensics and put the floor samples I had collected in the evidence cans." A sample from the burned area is put in one can and a control sample, taken from the other side of the room, goes into the other. Scientific analysis would be done in the lab to compare the samples. This would prove (or possibly dis-prove) his theory that someone set a trap for the woman – but why? What was the motive for her death?

Jurek set the phone down as he struggled to pull on a second pair of latex gloves; the first ones had split open. Even a size XL was a tight fit on his large sweaty hands. Careful to avoid cross contaminating the evidence with his DNA or prints, Jurek reached for the doorknob. "Jurek, are you still there? Hello?"

"Yeah, Cap. I don't want to mess up what looks like charred flesh on the knob. I had to put on a new glove before trying the door. Even the XL's are too small for me. Does anyone make a size XXL?"

"I don't know. I'll check with our supplier. Did the knob turn or was the door locked?"

"It turns easily, but the door won't open. I can't see anything wrong on the inside. I'm going around back to check the outside." Jurek walked to the rear of the structure. He couldn't avoid stumbling over pieces of old, junky furniture, discarded lumber and random scattered debris from the fire. Determined to figure out why the door would not open, he finally found his way, in the pre-dawn darkness, to the rear door.

Jurek was ready to try the doorknob from the outside to see if it would turn easily in his hand like it had on the inside. As he approached the door he couldn't believe what he saw it, "Holy shit, Cap.

There's a small garden shovel back here. It's wedged between the doorknob and the ground. It's enough to keep the door from opening. I'll send you a picture of it." The spade looked innocent enough, something that would not raise concern. It was about forty inches long from the blade to the handle. It was positioned in such a way to jam the door and keep it from opening. The blade of the spade was pushed about two inches deep into the soil. The handle had been wedged under the knob at a forty-five degree angle to the ground. "Its enough resistance to keep the door from opening. I'm also tagging the shovel for the forensic team."

Jurek had collected enough evidence to prove that the fire originated in the front room of the house and then followed a pre-set trailer to the rear. With the fire raging from the front to the rear and the back door blocked, the victim had nowhere to go. The woman was trapped by the shovel and was not able to escape the fire. The placement of that shovel was a material act that was involved in, and perhaps caused, the victim's demise.

"Good work, Jurek. I think we have what we need to get a homicide detective assigned to help us out." The case had migrated from fire investigation to an arson investigation, and now it had become a murder investigation.

Jurek came back to the front of the building and approached Lt. Craemer, "This 'dumb-ass cop' is declaring that this is now a crime scene. I'm taking over control to protect the chain of evidence that you and your 'dumb-ass' crew missed."

"Look, Rooky," said Craemer. "It ain't my job to look for evidence. That's your job. So don't pull that high and mighty stuff with me." Craemer knew that, even though it wasn't his job, Chief Sanchez expected his firefighters and investigators to work together. This was especially important in a death investigation. At least Craemer's crew found the body early on. In the first fire, his guys walked over the body a few times before they noticed it.

"I've called forensics to come in and investigate the scene. They should arrive in about an hour or so. I don't want to see your crew in the building unless I call them to take care of a re-kindle. Leave a hose connected to the hydrant, just in case there's a flare-up and I need to use it."

A "healthy" rivalry exists between firefighters and investigators and Jurek decided to throw his final jab. "Lieutenant, one more thing, I need to review the 'First In Reports' as soon as they are finished. Assuming, of course, they were actually filled out." Jurek had a hunch that the "First In Reports" had not been filled out.

Hot! In Tomales

A 'First In Report' is a standard form used by firefighters to collect their observations and record activities performed by the crew once they arrive on scene. Jurek was interested in the answers to a few of the questions on the form such as:

- Were any obstacles found impeding access?
- Were exterior doors ajar or unlocked?
- Did you smell any unusual odors?
- Notice of unusual flame or smoke colors?

"Son-of-a-bitch, Grotowski..." said a dejected Craemer, knowing Jurek would win this. Frustrated and angry, Craemer walked back to the rig to pull his guys back. He was heard grumbling under his breath about all the "young-shit-know-it-alls" that seem to be joining the fire service today.

Jurek yelled after him, "I also want to see any pictures your guys may have taken of the crowd for this fire and the other two fires as well."

Jurek knew he would either need permission from the property owner or a search warrant to go back in and investigate the first two fires after the fact. Even though a few weeks had passed, he wanted to see if he could still detect accelerants, fire patterns or anything else that might link the fires together. He would also take a close look at the exit doors to see if they were jigged up like this one was. If Jurek could find patterns, it would establish the fact that a serial arsonist was responsible for the fires. Time is the enemy of fire investigation; the longer the time span between knocking the fire down and investigating it, the more difficult it is to find the evidence needed to prove arson.

Jurek had consumed a few beers at last night's retirement party. He needed to relieve himself – soon. The early morning chill made matters worse. Plus, he knew that he could not leave the scene unattended or risk losing the evidence. In one of his trips to Emmitsburg, Jurek learned about the need to preserve the chain of evidence. In the case of Michigan vs. Tyler, the U.S. Supreme Court upheld a landmark decision by the lower courts that had ruled *"if custody of a crime scene was broken, for any reason, even for a few minutes, evidence found after the break would not be admissible in court."* The scene was defined as the physical structure and the immediate land upon which it sits.

But still, nature was calling and that call was getting louder. Jurek could not hold it much longer. The Marin County Fire Station in Tomales was just a half-mile away, on Dillon Beach Road, but Jurek knew he could not leave the scene. He had no choice but to go outback and find relief under an Italian plum tree. He did follow the letter of the law by not leaving the property. Jurek was now ready to focus on his job and continue his watch over the scene while waiting for the forensics team to arrive.

Jurek called Captain Dibdall again, "Hi Cap. Can you arrange to have a deputy come to maintain the scene? Once someone is here to maintain the watch, I'll be able to go back to the first two fires to see if they were set intentionally too."

"Okay. I'll call dispatch and ask that someone be sent out as soon as possible."

"Thanks, Cap. I can't help but think that Rollins must have missed something, accelerants, jammed doors, or even burn trails. If we find there's a similar MO between these fires..."

"I'm following you Jurek, good thinking. We'll be able to show the evidence that proves we have a serial arsonist."

"Exactly, Cap."

"Keep me posted on what you find, Jurek," said Dibdall. "I've worked with Lieutenant Forrest in the Sheriffs Office for years. He's a good man, kinda' old school, but a damn good cop. Right now he's down two detectives but I'll set up time for the two of us to meet with him and go over the evidence anyway. Maybe he's got an ace up his sleeve and can shake someone loose to work with us."

Chapter 4

The sun had risen into a dense, early morning marine layer. The microclimates in Western Marin County typically start with cool mornings, especially in the fall, with fog, lots of fog. It was early, about seven in the morning, and Jurek sat in his truck struggling to keep his eyes open. He had now been awake for nearly twenty-four hours and was anxious to get home and get some rest. *Where in the hell is the forensics team? They should have been here by now.*

Another hour passed when finally, the forensics team pulled up. The Medical Examiner for Marin County was with the team. He introduced himself to Jurek, "Good morning, I'm Doctor Jonah Chiang, the county ME. We're here to bag some evidence and remove the remains. Show us what ya' got."

"You guys must be really busy. Either that or ya' stopped for donuts and coffee." Jurek, normally polite, was harsh, probably due to exhaustion. "I called three hours ago. What took you so darn long to get here?" The look on Chiang's face was one of amazement at Jurek's insolence. It quickly turned to anger as he unloaded on Jurek.

"Listen pal. First off, we don't have the funding to staff on a seven by twenty-four basis. Plus, in case you've been asleep for the past four hours, the fog is very thick today and it slowed us down."

"Got it." Jurek said rather sheepishly. Chiang's response pinned Jurek's his ears back. Embarrassed, he apologized asking, "Could we start over?"

"Sure."

"Good morning, Doctor Chiang. My name is Jurek Grotowski. I'm the fire investigator on this case and I've been here since two in the morning."

"Great, good for you. Now stop the whining and tell me what you've learned about this case."

"Well, for starters, I found the remains of an elderly woman along with a ton of evidence that will prove her death was deliberately caused by arson. This is now a murder case, Doctor Chiang, and I'll show you why I believe that to be true."

"I accept your apology. Would you care for a donut?" Chiang's odd sense of humor is legendary.

"I'll grab one in a minute." There were no donuts but in that moment, Chiang realized that Jurek's sense of humor was on par with his own.

"Do you know for a fact that it's a woman?"

"Yes. Parts of her anatomy were visible. She's probably in her seventies. Let me take you to her."

"Sure. Let's take a look." As Jurek led Chiang through the house, he pointed out things he had noticed earlier; the teacups on the dining table, the kerosene cans, the oyster shells, the burn trailer and medicine bottles in the bathroom. Chiang stopped for a moment, taking a closer look at the medicine bottles. The label on the first bottle he picked up was but it appeared to be lorazepam. The intense heat had charred the labels and melted the plastic. Chiang tagged them with an identity flag so his team would be sure to take them back to the lab for analysis. They worked their way to the rear of the house, to the location near the back door where Jurek had found the body.

"The victim has certainly been crisped up by the heat. Her muscles have tightened, putting the body into what I call 'the pugilistic state.' She looks like a prize fighter in the ring."

"She went through hell before she died."

"You're right, Jurek. Is it ok to call you Jurek?"

"Sure. I mean, no. I mean it's fine if you want to call me Jurek." Jurek's lack of sleep was showing.

"This is the worst way to die. She suffered a lot before the lights went out. Show me what else you found. I'll have my team go over the area just to make sure we capture every bit of evidence that's here. I want to help you nail this guy."

"I found something on the doorknob," Jurek pointed it out for Chiang. "It looks like burnt flesh. Could your guys test it to see if it's from the victim? If it's her flesh then we'll know that she died trying to get out."

"Okay, sure, we'll test for a DNA *match*. No pun intended."

"What?" Jurek, too exhausted to catch Chiang's play on words, didn't get the joke.

"You know, a DNA 'match' as in the thing used to start fires." Chiang, one of the best Crime Scene Investigators in the country, was known for the odd quality and timing of his humor.

"I found a line of blisters on the linoleum floor that starts in the front room and goes to the rear. I scraped up some floor samples."

"Did you take a standard to compare it to?"

"Yes, I put the control sample in one can and a blister sample the other. I removed the kick molding and found wet, unlit kerosene behind it. I put a piece of the wood-soaked kerosene in the larger can. Hopefully the samples will prove it was a trailer."

"Sure. We will test 'em to see if the trailer was made with the same accelerant used in the main fire. It sure smells a like kerosene to me."

31

"I agree. I also noticed a kerosene smell in the kitchen. I want to show you something else, Doc, in the back yard." Jurek led Chiang around the outside of the house to the rear door. Pointing to the shovel he said, "This shovel was used to wedge the door shut. It kept the woman from escaping to safety. Can you check it for prints?"

"Sure. You've done a thorough job marking the evidence, Jurek. It makes our job a lot easier."

"Look, Doc. I'm sorry I came off like a jackass when you first got here. This is the third fire in five weeks and two people are dead because of them."

"No worries. I realize the pressure. We're here to help you. We need to work together."

"Thanks. Will your guys be here for a while?"

"We'll be here for at least another hour or so."

"I was back east when the first two fires were set. I want to go to them to see what I can find."

"Did you get permission from the owners to go back and investigate those scenes?"

"Yes. Dispatch contacted the owner. As it turns out, the same guy owns all three of the properties that were burned. He rents them out."

"Hmmm," Chiang mused, "do you think that's a coincidence or something more?"

"Don't know for sure, but I'm thinking it's more than a coincidence. It seems fishy to me."

Hot! In Tomales

"Go ahead and check those other structures out. We'll maintain the watch on this fire scene."

"They're nearby, only a couple of blocks away. I'll be back within the hour and catch up with you and discuss next steps."

Tomales, California is a small town, six square blocks in size. As Jurek drove to the scene of the other fires he noticed that the streets were empty. Deserted, the town appeared to be cloaked in an eerie sort of emptiness. There were no people to be found – anywhere. Nobody was out walking around. The Deli and General Store stood across the street from each other at the main intersection in Tomales. As Jurek drove by, he did not see anyone inside either business. *Strange.*

The sky lightened when the fog layer began to lift. The gloominess would last for a few more hours. Then, as happens in coastal regions, the day would turn bright with sunshine.

It didn't take Jurek long to get to the other fire scenes. He called Dibdall to check in and let him know where he was. "Cap, I'm at the scene of the first fire, the one on West Street."

"Jurek," said Dibdall, "an elderly woman died in that fire too but it was ruled an accidental death."

"I'm going to the rear first." It took Jurek about a minute, maybe two, to get to the backyard. Similar to house that burned last night it was in disrepair as well. The yard was littered with old furniture and overgrown vegetation. There was even an old rusted out Ford pickup truck with a license plate that was last renewed during Nixon's administration. "Holy smokes, Cap. There's a shovel lying near the back door of this place too." Jurek made note of it and took a picture. "There are marks in the soil that may have been made by the end of the shovel and I believe it was dug into the ground to jam this door too." *I have to get ahold of the first-ins for this fire.*

"Sounds very similar, Jurek, same MO. Likely done by the same guy. Could you ask Chiang if he can have his team sweep this scene too?"

"Oh man, Cap. Two kerosene cans were tossed into the back of an old pick-up in the backyard."

"Tag them and ask Chiang to check for prints."

"Will do. I'm going inside to see if anything else was missed in the initial investigation." Closed up since the fire, with minimal ventilation, once inside it was déjà vu for Jurek. "Wow, Cap. Even though it's diluted, I smell kerosene in here too. This fire started in the front room, just like the one last night. I pushed away some of the fall-down debris and found another trailer. It was used to push the fire to the rear of the house, to a second ignition point. Coincidentally, there are teacups on the kitchen table here too, just like in today's fire. I guess these ladies sure like their tea..."

"This guy's a pro, Jurek. He likes setting up two-stage fires. The first ignition blocks the path to the front exit of the house sending whoever is in there to the rear. Seconds later, about the time the victim gets to the rear, a second ignition takes place and traps them. With the exit blocked, they die; just like the woman you found this morning did. How could Rollins miss this much evidence?"

"How? Because, like I told you, he's worthless. Period. I'm just about done here and I plan to stop at the second fire next."

"Don't waste your time, Jurek. Rollins did not find anything to indicate arson and with no death, it was ruled accidental. The building was a safety risk so the owner had it razed."

"Wait, Doctor Chiang ruled the West Street fire accidental? But did he ever visit the scene?"

"No, he didn't. He determined the victim died from a heart attack," replied Dibdall.

"What about this place? Will West Street get razed too? Cap, we've got new evidence now."

"Jurek, the evidence from the West Street fire will help establish a serial arsonist is behind these fires. By showing your new evidence, we can get it declared a crime scene again. No worries."

"We now have evidence that proves both of the deaths are arson related. We need more time, Cap."

* * *

On his way back to the scene of this morning's fire, Jurek stopped at the Marin County Fire Station in Tomales. It was literally just around the corner. He called ahead and left a message asking for copies of "First-In" reports for each of the three fires. He wanted pictures taken of the onlookers at each fire too. Fire Investigators study crowd pictures hoping to find a face that may be common to multiple fires.

When Jurek arrived, except for the crew out back shooting buckets, the station looked deserted. The equipment bay was neat and orderly. Engine 12 had been washed and ready for service. The crew's turnout gear was laid out, ready for the next call.

As Jurek approached the office area in the rear of the building, he overheard Lt. Craemer talking on the phone. He heard him say, "Listen, Dibdall, your boy-wonder fire investigator wants me to hand over the first-ins plus the crowd pictures we have. That kid sure screwed up the evidence this time. Did you know he left the scene unattended without proper coverage? I'm not about to hand over any more stuff to him so he can it mess up."

Hot! In Tomales

When Craemer saw Jurek walk in, his jaw hit the floor. "For your information, Lieutenant, forensics is maintaining a watch at the scene so the chain of evidence is still intact. Now give me those 'First-In' reports I asked for – assuming your hose-jockeys actually filled them out. I also want copies of any pictures your guys may have taken."

"Well, ah..." Craemer knew he had been caught in a lie. "Just give me a few minutes to find them, Grotowski. I know they're here somewhere."

Craemer was an old school firefighter. A guy who enjoyed knocking down fires but didn't waste much time on procedure. He knew the reports did not exist. He also knew the correct procedure was to complete them at the scene or shortly after the crew leaves the scene. Important observations can be forgotten if completed too long after the incident.

"Look, Craemer, I know the reports don't exist. Don't make things worse by falsifying them."

"I have them, Rooky. Here they are." As Jurek read the reports, he noticed the ink was barely dry. Worse yet, Craemer had mistakenly dated them with today's date instead of the date the fires occurred. Jurek left with the First-In reports and a few crowd pictures. He knew that falsifying paperwork could be a big problem. *I have what I need to destroy this clown.*

Chapter 5

After his heated discussion with Craemer, Jurek drove back to the scene of today's fire so forensics could leave. He found Chiang out back sorting through a trash container. "Doctor Chiang, I visited the first fire and found similar evidence to what we have found here."

"Are you talking about the one on West Street?"

"Yes. May I ask why you are out here digging through the trash?"

"Clues, Jurek. I'm always amazed at the clues that end up in the trash. For example, did you know that someone who frequented this house had very small hands and feet? I found a pair of men's boots, size six – indicating really small feet. I also found a left-handed white glove – size small. The kind that a woman would wear to the opera."

"Do you think they were worn by the victim, Doctor Chiang?"

"No. I don't."

"What do you make of it then?"

"Well, for starters, they either belong to a small adult, maybe a little person, or a large child. Also, since they were near the top of the trash barrel, I assume they were tossed in recently."

"Do you think the victim threw them in there? Maybe she was just getting rid of old stuff."

"That could be. Or, the person who had worn them simply tossed them out."

"Perhaps trying to hide the fact that the person who owned them had ever been here?"

"Who knows? We may be dealing with a little person if they're the arsonists. What did you find?"

"The MO at West Street indicates that the same arsonist staged both fires. Striking similarities. Is it possible for you to send someone from your team over to officially assess the scene?"

"Sorry. Dispatch called a few minutes ago. A dead body was discovered over in Novato and we have to investigate." As Chiang turned to walk away, he stopped, turned and said, "Listen, Jurek, since we are only two blocks away, we'll investigate the West Street. The DB in Novato isn't going anywhere soon – I hope."

"You've already deemed the West Street victim died of natural causes, not arson. What evidence did your team discover when they found the body?"

"Jurek, we never investigated that fire. Rollin's report indicated that the fire was accidental and not arson related."

"How did the old lady die then?"

"The team found her dead in her bed. We took her remains to the lab to perform an autopsy. She had signs of heart failure with no sign of smoke in her lungs. Therefore, we figured she must have succumbed before the fire started."

"Interesting...so no smoke in the lungs indicates she died before the fire even started. Could the fire have triggered a heart attack?"

"Sure, but there should be smoke in her lungs."

"The MO at West Street seems to be identical. I smelled kerosene, and saw a trailer leading from the front of the house to the rear."

"Sounds like the same accelerant was used in both fires, kerosene. It's common out here."

"I found a small shovel near the back door too."

"Great job, Jurek. You don't miss much do you? The evidence is suggesting a serial arsonist..."

* * *

Sitting in his truck waiting for someone to come to watch the scene, Jurek thought back about events of the day. First, he had collected enough evidence to warrant extra resources from homicide to help investigate the arson related deaths. Second, the copies of the falsified "First-Ins" that Craemer created were concerning. Sure, paperwork is filled out days after a fire sometimes, but in this case the dates on the reports are wrong – evidence of fraud committed by Craemer. The reports could damage, or possibly put an end to his career. Finally, the most important event of the past twenty-four hours was reconnecting with Jenny...

Chapter 6

Jenny happened to be at the same bar where Parker's retirement party was held. Jurek's heart did flip-flops when he first saw her. She was there with seven work colleagues. Jurek watched from the other side of the bar, lacking the courage to approach her. Jenny looked hot in her skin-tight jeans, five-inch heels and a low-cut, cream-colored sweater. As she danced, her long auburn hair gently bounced atop her shoulders.

Jurek had noticed that a guy named Clint, one of the men in Jenny's group, was showing her a lot of interest. Jurek could see that she was flirting with him too. Maybe Clint was a bigwig in the firm or perhaps an important client. Either way, Jurek was convinced that Jenny didn't really want anything to do with this guy but had to play along. *Is Jenny pretending to flirt with Clint so as not to make any waves?*

Clint was draped all over Jenny at the pool table. *Trying to show her the proper way to hold a cue stick? Right.*

Hot! In Tomales

The drinks flowed freely and Clint became a lot chummier. Finally, he took her to the dance floor. It was a slow dance and the two were dancing close, so close that their bodies moved as one. Rage was building in Jurek. He wanted to bust this guy's head open and could have – he stood a good five inches taller than Clint. Jurek restrained himself, staying to his side of the room, still un-noticed by Jenny.

When firefighters celebrate anything, beer is usually present. The same old firehouse stories get told over and over – Jurek has heard them a hundred times. Tonight, his mind was focused on Jenny and Clint. Jurek had become more angered by the minute yet Jenny still had no idea that Jurek was in the bar. What really got him angry was that Jenny seemed to be totally into Clint.

When the third rendition of old "Shit I" had circled through the group of firefighters, Jurek's attention had completely shifted from the party to Jenny. As Clint drank more, he began getting more aggressive with her. He even tried to kiss her and began playing "grab ass" with her.

It was too much too fast for Jenny. She tried to get away from Clint but lost her balance and fell to the floor, she landing hard. Jurek, not seeing that she had fallen on her own, thought that Clint had pushed her.

That did it. Jurek ran across the bar to come to Jenny's aid. His adrenaline had kicked in and he slid across the pool table to where Clint was standing. He grabbed him by the scruff of the neck with one hand and stuck his other so far up the guy's rear end he could have charged him for a prostate exam. Stronger than a mule, Jurek lifted Clint up off the floor, carried him to the front door, and threw him out. He landed about four feet away on a pile of freshly filled trash bags. When Jurek went back to console Jenny, she was furious.

"Goddamit, Jurek. I can handle myself. That guy will probably take your butt to court. He's a partner in the law firm I work for."

"Nobody hurts my girl, Jenny. Nobody."

"But Jurek," Jenny said in a loud voice, "I'm not your girl...not anymore." She felt bad after saying that. Her words hurt Jurek. They had cut much deeper than she had intended.

"Listen, Jenny. If he tries to screw with me, both he *and his wife* will be up to their necks in fire code violations."

"That's it? That's all you got?" she asked. "Wife? Wait. Jurek, he told me he's not married."

"No. It's not all I got. And if he's not married, why does the SOB wear a goddam wedding ring?"

"I never noticed the ring."

44

Jurek, still shaking from the adrenaline rush had difficulty speaking. His words didn't flow well.

"Jurek, listen," said Jenny. "I didn't know that piece of crap was married."

"Fine," replied Jurek, still shaking a bit. Then he managed to ask Jenny, "Ya wanna dance?"

Jenny couldn't believe that Jurek asked her to dance. She was really pissed at him, and wanted to stay pissed for a while longer. He moved closer, put his arms around her and drew her close. She felt his large muscular chest. His arms reminded her of tree limbs. She gazed into his steel-blue eyes and her thoughts drifted back to when they were a couple. She couldn't help but remember the good times. The long talks by the fire, the walks on the beach, and of course, the nights they spent together... Jenny had a tough time after the break up and thought about him a lot.

Finally, she melted and said, "Sure, I'll dance with you, Jurek. Standing up or lying down?"

* * *

"Jurek, wake up." It was Doctor Chiang. "Hey, Pal. You were really out of it." Jurek forced himself to get moving and began packing up his gear. *The Sheriff's deputy should be here soon.* He called Jenny's cell

45

to let her know when he would be back. She did not pick up so he left a message. "Hey babe, this is your wake-up call. What time do you work today? Okay. I'll call you later." As soon as the deputy arrived on the scene, Jurek hopped in his truck to go home. He slept until three that afternoon.

* * *

The oyster shells he had found at the scene were haunting him, so he decided to visit someone who knew a lot about oysters, his grandmother, Juliana Grotowski. He knocked on her door at the Marin Assisted Living facility.

"Who's there?" she asked from behind a locked door inside of her apartment.

"Babcia, it's me, Jurek, your favorite grandson. I've stopped for a quick visit. I'm going to the store and want to check to see if you needed anything." She opened the door, but just a crack, to make sure it wasn't Gypsies trying to trick her.

"Jurek? You never visit, what's wrong? Is your father sick? Who died? Is it your mother? Is everyone okay?"

"No, Babcia." Babcia is Polish for Grandma. "It's all good. No one is sick. Do I need a special reason to pay a visit to my Babcia?"

46

Jurek made her feel at ease and she took the chain off the door to let him in. "Jurek. It's you. How are all of your children?"

"Babcia, you know I'm not married...not yet. No little ones either – at least that I know of."

"It's been months since you were here."

"Babcia, I was here last week." Juliana's memory had been failing, and was getting worse. He knew it wouldn't be long before his grandmother would no longer remember him at all. He was good about seeing her every week or so. "I'm on my way to the grocery to pick up a few things. Do you have a list? Is there anything I can get for you?"

"I don't want to be a burden, but I could use a few bananas; green ones, but not too green. I want them to ripen before God takes me. I'll pay you for them." Juliana, now in her late nineties, frequently voiced her desire to join her departed husband, Stanislaw, in heaven; at the same time, she wanted to be revived, "No DNR for me," she would say. "Keep me alive for a few days...then we'll see."

"Babcia, listen. Someday you will see Dziadek again, but for now, you have your family and friends here."

Jurek's grandparents came to this country years ago to work in the oyster business. He wanted to ask her about the oyster shells he had found in the

47

Loomis fire. "Tell me what it was like when you and Dziadek first came to this country." Jurek was amazed that she was able to remember things that happened fifty to sixty years ago with clarity. Her short-term memory was failing fast. Unfortunately she couldn't recall what she had for lunch that day.

"We came to U.S. from the old country back in nineteen thirty three. We found work in the oyster farms in ah...in ah... how do you say, marie land?"

"Babcia, you mean, Maryland?"

"Yes, yes. Maryland. We had worked fish farms back in Poland and had experience with oyster too." Aquaculture was well established in Poland, tracing back to the mid-seventeenth century. When Jurek's grandparents first came to the U.S., they worked the oyster farms of Chesapeake Bay. Later they moved to Louisiana for a while, before heading west to settle in the charming seaside town of Bodega Bay, California. It has since become a vacation haven with its many restaurants and beautiful views.

"What was the work like?"

"Very hard. We work very hard. We save every penny we can so we could buy a home overlooking the bay." They bought a modest home on the bluffs in Bodega Bay with a beautiful view of what is now Spud Point Marina.

"I thought you lived in Tomales Bay, Babcia?"

"Yes, we did, but my husband wanted to live far away from work, away from smell. We lived there for a few years before we got our house."

Tomales is an agricultural community made up of hard-working families. Many of the locals had also worked the oyster harvest operations along the banks of Tomales Bay. When Jurek's grandparents first arrived on the west coast, the oyster business was in its infancy. Soon the demand for oysters began growing in markets along the West Coast. The business grew and the elder Grotowski's had been instrumental in its development.

"Tell me Babcia, why would someone have a meal of just oysters?"

"Well," she thought for a moment, "Because they taste good? Or maybe they thought they had strong cure powers."

"Strong cure powers?"

"Sure, Jozef. People think oysters cure disease."

Jurek was confused. To make matters worse she called him Jozef – the name of his brother.

"Tell me, Babcia," testing her memory, "What did you have for lunch?" Jurek knew from the bulletin board that they had served chicken and rice.

"We had ham. It was good. You want some?"

Chapter 7

The Johnson home was quiet. Slivers of sunlight sifted in between the slats in the mini blinds as the day's light began oozing in along the edges of the heavy draperies. It was one of those lazy December mornings with nothing on the calendar, no reason to get out of bed. "Mark," she said using a quiet, almost whisper-like voice, "I really love having you home with me, I wish we could stay right here forever." Chao-Xing nudged her husband to wake him. Moving closer she rubbed his calf with her toes as she whispered in his ear, this time using a deeper, sultrier voice, "Hey, Fabio. Do you want to mess around a little?"

"Chao, it's too early...and what about Cory?" asked a groggy Mark Johnson.

"Babe, it's almost eight-thirty and Cory's off to school. He left twenty minutes ago." Chao was a morning person. Her routine was to get up early and start on her activities for the day. Typically, she would have the laundry started and breakfast on the table by now. But this was not a typical day. She woke with a desire burning deep within, a fire that only her man could extinguish. Chao wanted to share this moment with him – she was anxious for him, she was ready for him.

"Let me see now," pondered Johnson thinking about her offer, "Do I want to mess around? You mean with you?" Johnson was kidding of course.

"I sure hope so," she said, inching closer while kissing the area of his neck just beneath his ear. Gently nibbling on the outside of his ear lobe she then teased the inside of his ear with her tongue and said, "Mark, we've got the whole house to ourselves today; nothing on the calendar. We could stay in bed and do this all day long."

"I love it when Cory leaves for school early," he said, coming to full attention. He turned to Chao and gazed into those dark, captivating eyes of hers, eyes that could see into his heart and cut through all of his bullshit – they could see down into his soul.

"Me too," giggled Chao.

"How about coming over to the dark side?" She knew exactly what he meant and was more than happy to comply. Sliding on the slick satin sheets she moved a few inches closer.

"How's that, Fabio? Close enough?"

"Perfect, Babe. You'll be glad you came for a visit. I've got a 'little something' for you."

"I can't wait," said Chao with that giggle of hers. Johnson maneuvered his arm placing it under her neck, bringing her even closer. His hands massaged her back, slowly. She responded by reaching for him. Johnson's hands soon found their way under the silks of her nightclothes. Gently, and ever so slowly, he slipped them off of her. The morning sun had become more intense, flooding the room with light, as she exposed her everything to him. She met him with a deep kiss. He knew she was ready for him, and she knew that he was ready for her.

"Shit," he said as his phone started buzzing.

"Dammit, Mark. Don't answer that...please, not right now. Call whoever it is back in a few minutes."

Mark Johnson was a thirty-year veteran with the Marin County Sheriff's Office. He had worked the homicide desk for the past ten years and during that time he had solved a number of high-profile cases that won him praise. His crime solving techniques, along with his ability to speak in front of audiences, made him a popular choice on the lecture circuit.

Johnson had cracked a bizarre case involving radioactive material that ended up in the hands of radical terrorists. The U.S. government had dumped the material in the waters off of the Farallon Islands at the end of the Second World War. Johnson was shot in the line of duty and had been recuperating at home for the past ten weeks.

Even though his wounds had healed, his doctors were reluctant to give him the official "OK" to go back to full time duty. They felt that because Johnson was nearly sixty years old, he would require a longer recovery period. But the longer Johnson stayed home, the more he enjoyed being away from the homicide desk. In fact, he actually began to consider retiring permanently. He was ready to live the lifestyle he had worked so hard to achieve.

Johnson and is wife, Chao-Xing, had reignited their relationship and became inseparable. They did everything as a couple. Even though Chao felt this was a little stifling, she had nearly lost him once and was pleased, and proud, to have him with her. Then, in a contrary moment, Johnson grabbed the phone.

"Mornin', Mark. Forrest here." Chao could hear the booming voice of Johnson's boss, Lt. Denny Forrest. "Say, Mark. I was wondering if you could come up to the office later today, around one or so? We all miss you up here Mark." Johnson had not gone back to the Sheriff's Office since the shooting. "Billy Dibdall, the Fire Marshall, will be here to present evidence on a couple of recent fire-related deaths over in Tomales, in Western Marin."

"I've read about the fires in Tomales, Lieutenant – awful." Johnson cast a glance at Chao's face. She was not happy.

"It sits about five miles from Tomales Bay, near Bodega Bay. Way the hell out in cow country," said Forrest. The rocky hills in that area could never sustain deep-root crops, so grass covers the fields. It made for a good grazing area for cows and sheep.

"Like I said, I've read about those fires. But, Denny, you're aware that I haven't been cleared for active duty yet, right?"

"Come on, Mark. I don't want you to come back to work – not until you're ready that is. I was hoping that you could help us review the evidence. It's a one-and-done deal, that's it. I guarantee it's nothing more than that. Mark, what'da ya say?"

Lt. Forrest had gone above and beyond in the weeks following Johnson's shooting. He made sure that his family was taken care of during his long recuperation. In fact, it was Denny Forrest who convinced the county to keep Johnson at full pay and benefits. He also made sure that Chao and their three kids each received counseling. There was no way Johnson could possibly say no to him.

"Sure, Denny, I guess... You said one o'clock?" Chao's heart sank when she heard him say that. She was not prepared for him to go back to work.

Hot! In Tomales

"Yes, one o'clock. Thanks, Mark. See you then. Come up earlier if you want to do lunch."

Smoke was pouring from Chao's ears. She was livid. "Mark, what the hell? You can't go back to work yet; you're not ready. And you know what? I'm not ready either. I want you to stay here, at home with me, for a long, long time. I almost lost you once and I don't want to go through that again." The memories of Johnson in his hospital bed were fresh in her mind. Tears flowed down her cheeks as she told him, "For the love of God, Mark. You almost died."

"Chao, I love you and I don't want to hurt you." Wanting to comfort her, he reached to draw her close to him.

Chao figured Johnson was purely interested in finishing what they started. She snapped, "Forget it mister. That damn homicide desk is on your mind. Not me." With that, Chao got out of the bed and stormed from the room, knocking over a table lamp in her haste, leaving Johnson lying there alone with his desires.

* * *

Johnson had always worn his hair long, but after being off for a few weeks he began to look down right scruffy. He refused to tie his hair in a pony tale or wear a cap. It was a warm day for December so he drove with the top down on his gold Porsche Boxster. He enjoyed the feeling of his hair flowing in the breeze – it made him feel alive. The traffic on the 101 was heavy. It was a few minutes before his one o'clock meeting by the time Johnson pulled into an open parking spot in the congested parking lot at the Marin County Sheriff's Office

"Mark," Sally Tomms called out, when she saw him step out of his car. "Mark, you're looking great. Welcome back." Sally, returning from lunch, was the head of Marin County Family Services.

"Thanks Sally, it's been a while."

As he hurried into the Sheriff's building Johnson ran into Eddie Dalton. Eddie has been the county chopper pilot forever. "Mark. Wow, it's really good to see you, man. How are you feeling?"

"Better, Eddie; better every day, thanks. Have you been doin' much fishin' lately?" Eddie loved to fish and had often asked Johnson to join him. "I might want to take you up on your offer to go fishing one of these days."

"Just let me know when..."

Johnson had known these folks for years. They were all part of his work family. This was Johnson's first visit to the Sheriff's office since the shooting and his co-workers were glad to see him. A small crowd quickly gathered to wish him well as he made the walk down the main hallway...it was the closest to a "hero's welcome" he had ever experienced.

Everybody that saw him greeted him with warm wishes and a personal comment or two. They were all truly happy to see him, and they were especially pleased to see that his injuries were on the mend.

In that one moment, with everyone praising his accomplishments and speaking so kindly about him, Johnson realized that he had been specially blessed. Over the years he had worked with a great group of people. Many were good friends and others knew of him through the endless stories told by others. *What if I hadn't survived the shooting? Is this what my wake would have been like? I'll miss these people...*

Johnson continued down the hallway toward Forrest's office. As he passed by the departmental trophy case he noticed the white pine woodwork was old and needed a new coat of varnish. Johnson had walked by it for years, but never took the time to look at what was in the display case. The plaques were dusty and dated from years long since passed. He stood there for a minute observing history.

His eyes were drawn to the two awards not yet caked with dust; they were new and recently added. One was a Medal of Honor posthumously awarded to Sargent Thomas Bartlett. Tommy had been Johnson's partner for eight years. Tears welled up in his eyes as he recalled the events that had claimed Tommy's life. He was shot to death at pointblank range while the two were on a stakeout. Tommy never regained consciousness after being shot. He died in Johnson's arms.

The other new plaque in the trophy case was also a Medal of Honor – this one was dedicated to Johnson himself. The story on the plaque outlined the valiant efforts and leadership he exhibited on a recent tri-county task force. The task force had discovered and then foiled a plot by Middle-Eastern terrorists to build a dirty bomb. The case itself had instantly become one of legend. It was known as, "The Secret of the Farallones."

Johnson stood there, thinking about the history in that trophy case when someone walked up from behind. "Mark." said a familiar voice, "Congrats on that Medal of Honor, man. You earned it." Johnson recognized the voice of his longtime friend and colleague, Dr. Jonah Chiang. Chiang had been the Marin County Medical Examiner for ten years.

"Hey, Jonah. Thanks. What've you been up to? It's been a long time."

"Come on, Mark, you've always been a drama-queen – even back in high school." Johnson and

Chiang became friends when they were freshmen at Lowell High School. "It's only been ten weeks. How are Chao and the kids?"

"The family's fine. Thanks for asking."

"Are you here to apply for a job? We have a few openings on the homicide desk. You might actually qualify for them," it was Chiang humor at its best.

"No. I'm not here to apply for a job. Forrest called and asked if I would come up to review some evidence discovered in a recent fire."

"Oh, probably the Tomales fire, or rather fires, Mark. I walked the scene with the fire investigator a couple of days ago; a young man with a great sense for fire science. He's dead nuts sure that this case is murder by arson; possibly even a serial arsonist."

"What do you think, Jonah? Is he right?"

"Why don't you look at the evidence first, Mark. Then I'll tell you what I think."

"Fair enough, Jonah. I'll stop by after I meet with Forrest. I've got something personal I'd like to discuss with you."

"Sure. If I'm not in my office, I'll be in the lab. I'm looking forward to catching up with you."

Chapter 8

Mark Johnson prided himself on being punctual; usually arriving early. He knocked on Forrest's door. "You're early," Forrest said, tongue in cheek, as he opened the door. Forrest's office was exactly how Johnson remembered it. There were a few pieces of industrial style furniture, and a file cabinet. His desk, sitting in front of the window, was flat and bare, without drawers. The leather chair had a few wear-spots on it. The whiteboard was next to the. There was nothing on the walls; no artwork – not even a calendar. Johnson saw Billy Dibdall and couldn't help but notice a mountain of a man talking him. Forrest went on, "I'm glad you could make it, Mark. How ya' doin?"

"I'm doing ok Denny. Thanks for asking."

"Mark," Denny said as they walked over to Billy, "I'd like to introduce you to Jerzy Grotowski. He's the fire investigator for Marin County and of course, you've worked with Billy a number of times."

"Detective Johnson, I'm excited to finally get to meet you in person. You're a living legend. I've had the good fortune to attend your Crime Investigation lectures. Please, could you call me Jurek, sir?" Jurek was visibly nervous and excited to meet Johnson as he reached out to shake his hand.

"Thank you," said Johnson, noticing the size of Jurek's hand – it was huge. "It's good to meet you too...ah, Jurek is it?" Johnson turned to Dibdall. "Hey, Billy. How's it going for ya?"

"Can't complain Mark, but the bigger question is how are *you* doing? You gave us all a pretty big scare a few weeks back ya' know; getting shot by that bastard and all. It had to be awful."

Johnson and Dibdall had worked together on a number of cases over the years. "Thanks, Billy. I'm getting back to normal, slowly, whatever that means. So, Jurek," Johnson said, changing the focus of the conversation back to Jurek, "Lieutenant Forrest tells me that you have evidence proving that someone's killing with fire. I've read brief accounts of these fires in SFGate. Could you take a minute and tell me what you've found so far."

"That's why we're all here," said Forrest. "To review the evidence. Let's start. Go ahead, Jurek."

"Okay, thanks Lieutenant Forrest. For starters, we've had three fires in the town of Tomales over the passed few weeks. Does anyone know what the odds are of having three coincidental structure fires in a town of just two hundred people?"

"I would guess it's pretty darn low."

"Right, Detective Johnson. There are more than seventy thousand structures across the entirety of Marin County. Over the past five years, we have averaged just twenty-five structure fires per year."

"That's very impressive." Johnson said. "Looks like all of your Fire Prevention efforts have paid off over the years, Billy. Nice work."

"Right," said Dibdall, "Okay, you've all had a chance to read Jurek's report. This is a good time to ask him questions."

"I'll bite," said Johnson. "Jurek, could you take a minute and explain the most important piece of evidence that you found?"

"Well, I know that in each fire an accelerant was used. The crime lab confirms that the accelerant in two of the fires was kerosene. And, as it turns out, kerosene was also the accelerant used to direct the path of the fires."

"But Jurek, isn't kerosene common in Western Marin? The surface bedrock makes it impractical to pipe natural gas underground so the people in those parts use kerosene or liquid petroleum for heat."

"Yes, Detective Johnson, that's true."

Hot! In Tomales

"So if its common for people to use kerosene as an alternative to natural gas, how do you know that it was a unique accelerant for these fires?"

"Great question, Detective," said Jurek. "People in those parts use a lot of kerosene and its available at a lot of places for anyone who wants to buy it."

"Exactly, Jurek. So I guess my next question is this: how did you establish that an arsonist caused these fires just because kerosene was present? And what did you mean when you said it was used to *'direct the path'* of those fires?"

"By itself, the use of kerosene isn't so important, Detective; but *how* it was used is critical. Let me answer your second question first. A skilled arsonist is capable of setting up what we call a trailer. It will *direct* the fire to a secondary point of origin. Think of the trailer as a fuse. The lab tests concluded that the fuse in our fires was a trail of kerosene. It directed the fire from the front of the house to the rear."

"How in the hell can you prove that?" asked Johnson. "Is there evidence to back this up or is it just a theory at this point?"

"I found 'blisters' on the linoleum flooring."

"Blisters?" asked Johnson. "Please go on."

"The arsonist laid a kerosene trailer along the edge of the hall connecting the front of the house to the back – down where the wall meets the floor. As the kerosene burns it mars the floor. In this case, since the floor is linoleum the heat of the burning kerosene trailer raised blisters along the floor next to the wall. You can see it if you know what to look for. I took floor samples to the forensics lab and their tests proved conclusively that it was kerosene used for the trailer."

"Tell him what else was found to prove that kerosene was used."

"Sure, Cap. I lifted the toe-plate along the wall in the hallway and found a wet substance behind it. I also lifted a piece of the wood flooring in the front room and found moisture under it too. The lab tests proved that the moisture I found was kerosene. It had soaked through the crevices in the wood but never ignited because it was oxygen starved."

"OK, Jurek. You've convinced me that there is an arsonist at work out there and he likes to use kerosene, but how did you establish an intent to commit murder?" asked Johnson.

"It was the shovels," replied Dibdall.

"Wait. Shovels?" Johnson's head was spinning.

Dibdall began to explain. "Jurek found that the rear doors in both structures had been jammed shut with small garden shovels. It was these shovels that kept the victims from escaping."

"What the...?" replied Johnson.

"Yes, Detective. I found that a shovel was used to jam the rear door shut at the most recent fire. In fact, it was still in place when I arrived on the scene. I tried to open the door from inside and even with my size, I couldn't open it."

"I sent Jurek back to the first fire to see what he could find there," said Dibdall.

"Was it the same set-up Jurek?"

"Yes, Detective Johnson. At the scene of the first fire, on West Street, I found an identical shovel lying outside the rear door. Plus, I found marks in the dirt where the shovel would have been jammed in to keep the door from opening. Each of the fires killed someone."

"That's incredible, Jurek."

"I know, Detective Johnson. The killer had set two-stage fires. The first stage started in the front of the house blocking any escape that way." Johnson wrote down Jurek's comments in his notebook.

"Right," said Johnson. "Then what?"

"Before the victim could get to the rear exit, the trailer kicked off a second fire."

"So the victim got caught between the two fires?" Johnson added this to the whiteboard. "With the rear doors jammed by the shovels, there was no way to escape. So it appears that both women perished the same way?"

"Well, not exactly," said Jurek. "Dr. Chiang told me the actual cause of death for the first victim was a heart attack – not complications from the fire."

"Poor woman," said Johnson. "So how did the arsonist get into those buildings to lay down the trailers and set the fires?"

"Have you ever been to Tomales, Detective? It's very small with a handful of rundown homes. Main Street consists of four buildings. The Continental Inn, an old hotel, is on one corner. The General Store and Post Office are across the street. A small deli sits kitty-corner across the street from the Inn."

"That's it?"

"That's it. The town is so small there's not even a gas station. Everybody knows everybody else. These two houses had old style locks; the kind that can be opened with a skeleton key. I was able to find the door locks in the debris and opened them with the skeleton key I carry with me."

"Got it. So you're saying that the arsonist, or anyone else for that matter, could essentially just waltz right in, unnoticed?"

"Right. The other factor is that both of the victims were old and possibly hearing impaired – they may not have heard anyone enter."

"Thanks, Jurek. Good stuff. Let's review the facts we have and then move on to what we need to learn to solve the case." Denny was pleased to see Johnson taking charge. He was hoping to get him back to work soon and this case might help.

"Detective Johnson, I remember a lecture you gave entitled, 'No Unsolvable Crimes' in which you explained that to solve any murder case one must identify the means, the motive and the opportunity."

"Very good, Jurek," said Johnson. *I like this guy.*

"I think we've nailed the means," said Jurek. "Both fires were pushed with kerosene and a shovel jammed the rear door preventing escape."

"What else do we know?" asked Johnson.

"Well, three fires in a few weeks time were more than coincidence. At least two of the fires were set intentionally."

"Right, Denny. What else?" Johnson asked.

"Both of the victims were elderly women, Mark, and each of the fires was a two-stager with a trailer."

"Billy, that's good. What else? Anyone?"

"We know that there is a Marin County Fire Station literally around the corner – less than a quarter-mile away," said Jurek. "Maybe the arsonist had a score to settle with the county and decided to set these fires right under their noses."

"Interesting, Jurek," said Johnson. "Let's spend a couple of minutes and list what we don't know about the opportunity and motive."

"Is there some sort of a connection between the two women?" Dibdall asked.

"Is the arsonist working alone, or is he a hired flame, so to speak?" asked Forrest.

"That's a great question," said Johnson. "Did someone want them dead? Did that someone hire an arsonist?"

"All three properties were owned by..."

"Wait a minute, I must a' missed the fact that there were three buildings burned."

"Yes," said Jurek. "Only two of the buildings had fatalities. The first was demolished before we could do a thorough investigation."

"I see."

"Assuming the same person set both fires, was he after the properties and the two women were unfortunately collateral damage?"

Good question, Jurek," said Johnson. "Another question is this; is there something unique to the properties themselves?"

The discussion continued for another forty-five minutes before the energy slowed to a crawl. At that point Forrest said to the group, "We've had a good session today. Thanks for the great involvement everybody. My office will definitely be helping with the investigation." Then he said to Johnson, "Mark, can you stay for a minute after the others leave?"

Hot! In Tomales

As the others were leaving, Johnson prepared himself for the classic Denny Forrest sales pitch. All day long, Johnson was thinking that Forrest wanted him back to lead the investigation. *Why else would he call me in?* He also knew that going back to active duty would be very hard for Chao to accept. Johnson loved working homicide, and this case was dripping with intrigue, the kind of a challenge he craved. However, Johnson loved Chao more than the job and had already decided to decline Forrest's offer...but it never came. Instead Forrest shook Mark's hand and sincerely thanked him for his years of service also thanked him for taking the time to help out. "Mark, you're one of the best. Thanks. Keep in touch, will ya?"

As Johnson left, a wave of remorse washed over him. *Will this be my last time at Headquarters?*

Dr. Chiang was working in the lab titrating some sort of a colored liquid when Johnson found him. "Hey, Jonah. Got a sec?"

"Sure, Mark. What'd you think about the case Grotowski is trying to make?"

"I agree with him, Jonah. It's a case of murder, pre-meditated murder, using fire. He's done a great job establishing the means by which the deaths took place. Now, what's needed are a motive and a list of people with opportunity."

"So, Mark, you're coming back to work?"

"Jonah, no. I never said that."

"Sure sounded like you did. Mark, this case, this *job*, it's in your blood. I know you and I know you can't walk away from it."

"But it would really rip up Chao and I can't do that to her. Hell, Jonah, I *won't* do that to her."

"Mark, Chao, more than anyone else on this planet, knows what being a detective means to you. She may be mad as hell if you go back to work, but she knows better than to stand in your way."

"Jonah," Mark said after a long pause, "The problem is that I don't know if *I'm* ready, or for that matter, if I'm even capable of going back to active duty."

"What in the hell do you mean by *that*, Mark?"

Chapter 9

It was late in the afternoon, about three-thirty or so, when Johnson returned home from his meeting with Forrest. The late day shadows of December would soon meld into total darkness. The house was quiet as the final rays of a western sun were dancing playfully with dust particles suspended in air. Facing west, the kitchen has the final view of the sun before it sinks into the horizon. Today's sunset was an intricate palette of sky-blue pink colors.

As he was admiring the sunset Johnson started making a cup of tea. He put a mug of water into the microwave. It rotated on the plate until the timer rang. He never got the hang of making tea like Chao did. She was traditional Chinese and made it with the actual leaves. Johnson used premade tea bags. After the bag steeped for a few minutes in the hot water he added two sugar cubes and carefully carried the cup to his backyard Tea Garden. Mark Johnson is a man who enjoys solitude and was looking forward to spending a few minutes sitting in the garden to reflect on his meeting with Lieutenant Forrest. He hadn't noticed that Chao was sitting on the garden bench under the grape arbor. He was startled when she spoke, "So, when do you start?"

"Jeez, Chao. Ya' scared the bejesus out of me." After a pause, Johnson asked, "Start what?"

"I know you're going back to detective work again, Mark. I'm just wondering what the date will be so I can plan a nice going away party for you." Chao's voice was unusually calm and measured, so much so that it scared Johnson.

"Come on, Chao, a going-away party? Isn't that a little over the top, even for you?" Right after he said that, Johnson regretted it.

"Might as well make it a formal sendoff, Mark. That last case of yours almost ended you, and your girlfriend, the 'Bolinas Bitch', almost put an end to us. I can't deal with that kind of drama again, Mark. No. I *refuse* to deal with it again."

Here it comes. Chao has held her anger inside; bottled up for weeks. "Look Chao. First of all, nothing happened with that woman. That's the God's truth and you know it. Second, I didn't say 'yes' to Forrest."

"But did you say 'no' to Forrest? Hell, I don't think you're even capable of saying 'no' to Forrest. That man has you wrapped around his little finger."

"Well," Johnson said, kind of squirming around in his seat. "He never really asked, Chao. However, from the way he was acting it felt as though he really wanted me back. He's short-handed and needs to find someone to help out on an arson case."

"But why does it have to be you, Mark? I don't buy the notion that you're the only person in the whole wide world capable of solving this crime. He has always banked on you returning, Mark. That's why he never tried to fill your position, or Tommy's for that matter."

"I don't know why he hasn't filled those open jobs, Chao. I'm guessing there's some sort of budget issue looming. There always is. And of course, he's paying me full pay while I'm sitting at home."

"Did you happen to see your old friend, Jonah?"

"I did run into Jonah. I spoke with him after I met with Forrest. He said to say 'hi' to you."

"How's good old Jonah doing? Still single?"

"He's fine; and yes, he's still single. Why would you ask that?"

"Just a thought...maybe the two of you could share an apartment together in San Rafael. It would save you both a lot on your commute times."

"Chao, the past ten weeks have been difficult. I was gut-shot. It's painful and I'll have to deal with the lasting damage for the rest of my life. At the

73

same time, and with your help, I've been sober since the shooting. Neither of these are easy burdens by themselves. It's just been really difficult for me."

"So, poor you, Mark...poor you. Do you want to know what I've been dealing with? Do you?"

"Well, ah...sure Chao. I'd really like to know what you're going through."

"Cory had a tough time after we found you on the kitchen floor two months ago; bleeding, half dead, and full drunk. He never knew about your past and he still refuses to admit that his Dad's an alcoholic. He adores you, Mark. He's convinced that I made the whole thing up."

"I'll talk to him, Chao. He needs to know you are the one person who stood by me over the years and helped me get through the tough times."

"It's not just Cory. The girls had a hard time learning you're not invincible, that you could die. They're older and more understanding, and they're able to accept your failures. Still, it rattles them to think that your genes may affect them someday. At the market, the old Chinese women point and talk behind my back. I know what they're saying – for God's sake, don't they know I speak Mandarin? They call me 'Huài qīzi,' the bad wife. A wife that can't control her man."

"Chao, I'm sorry. I didn't know."

"Stop, Mark. I'm not done yet. Every time your overbearing mother comes to visit, I need to spend time consoling her because her little boy, her pride and joy, almost died. She should be consoling me."

"Chao..."

"But the worst of all, Mark Johnson, is that we have not made love in ten weeks. I long for your touch, your embrace, your kisses...and we finally had the opportunity this morning and you chose to talk to Forrest instead." Johnson just sat there with a dumbfounded look on his face. He was trying to think about how to say what he wanted to say; then, it just came out.

"Chao, I've decided it's time to retire. Believe me, it's not because you're against the idea of me doing police work. I love you, Chao, and I will never do anything to hurt you; but there are other reasons..." That grabbed her attention. She had the ability to look through his eyes, to see deep into his soul. The man of her dreams was standing in front of her willing to give up his career for her. She started to melt...but just a little. Johnson went on, "I met with Jonah today and described the nightmares I've been having; awful dreams about the shooter. Jonah thinks it's PTSD and suggested that I get some professional help."

"What are you talking about? What dreams?"

"I didn't want to bother you with it, Chao, but just about every night he's there, in my head."

"Who's there, Mark?"

"The shooter. The truth is, Chao, I'm *afraid* to go back to the homicide desk. I'm afraid the next guy won't miss."

"The shooter's dead, Mark. He'll never hurt you or anyone else, ever again. Besides, I've never known you to be afraid of anything before."

"I lost my edge, Chao. I was hung-over and in a fog. I should have been ready for him, but I wasn't."

"Mark, listen, you're the strongest person I have ever known. I also realize that I could be a widow right now – and it scares me. I'm not quite ready for that." Chao knew this conversation was hard on him so she tried to lighten the mood a bit. "Don't get me wrong. I'm still pretty hot and could find a man easy enough, but I'll never find anyone that could fill me with desire the way you do."

"Chao, is there another man?"

"No. Don't be stupid. I'm saying that I could never replace the feelings I have for you and only you. Feelings I've had since the first day we met."

"Chao, I could never replace my love for you either."

"Mark, you need to talk to someone about these dreams. Jonah's right, it sure sounds like you have

PTSD." Chao wrapped her arms around him and held him close to her. He couldn't hold back his emotions any longer and he began to sob. She held him and whispered in his ear, "I love you, Fabio."

"If I retire, Chao. Maybe we could take time to travel the world, like you've wanted to do for years."

"That would be nice. In another year Cory will be able to take care of himself, as long as we leave enough pizzas in the freezer." They sat in the garden, in each other's embrace, for a long time.

* * *

The next morning, Lt. Forrest called Johnson's cell. "Mark, I'm going to give this to you straight – I need you to come back, even if it's part-time. I'm short handed and you know how long it takes to find, hire and train a replacement."

"Denny, listen. I'm just not confident that I can manage an investigation anymore. I want you to know that Chao and I appreciate all you've done for us. But I have to say no thanks."

"Mark, I respect your feelings but damn it man. I need help and you know the ropes better than anyone. Listen, I've been given the 'OK' from the top brass to extend a job offer to Paula Chen."

"Are you serious?"

"I sure am."

"What makes you think she would want to leave the San Francisco homicide desk and come work in Marin?"

"Well, for starters, I heard through the grape vine that San Francisco PD has decided to move her off the homicide desk and put her on a permanent desk job. She'll never work homicide again...at least not for the City of San Francisco."

"Is she aware of that, Denny?"

"I think she's been told."

"Is it ok if I talk to her about it? I mean the job you want to offer her."

"Sure, go ahead. Tell her that I want her on my team. She'll be welcomed whenever she's ready. She'll start out working with you on the arson case."

"But, Denny. I just told you I'm not coming back." No response from Forrest. "Wait a minute, does my decision affect whether you hire Paula or not?"

"You bet it does. If you don't come back, she's SOL, Mark. I need you for one more case. I need time to find your replacement."

"You prick. You're using Chen as a pawn to get me back. Damn you, Denny." Johnson cut off the call with Forrest. Livid, he began walking the two short blocks from his house to Golden Gate Park.

Hot! In Tomales

The walk took him past Durty Nelly's Tavern. Johnson had been an alcoholic for as long as he could remember and the urge for a good, stiff drink was strong. He started drinking when he was fifteen years old. The euphoria of that first drink gave him a never-before-felt feeling. He was finally a man and his insecurities had disappeared at least that is, until he sobered up. Eventually the good feelings stopped but his never-ending thirst for alcohol continued. Johnson battled alcoholism his entire life. But he had been winning. And even though he fell off the wagon a couple of months ago, with Chao's help and his weekly AA meetings, he climbed back on and had been sober for the past two months.

Nelly's door was open. The crew was cleaning up. The smell of stale cigarette smoke and spilled drinks captivated him. He saw the old tables, chairs and familiar bar stools. *Just one won't hurt.* Then he remembered what Chao had told him about Cory not wanting to accept that his Dad was weak.

He called his sponsor, James Tarrtive. "James. Pick up," said Johnson. There was no answer. James couldn't answer. He was passed out on his living room floor and couldn't help.

Johnson had to dig deep. He said a prayer and found the strength to keep walking, to keep going, and most importantly, to not give in. He knew that if he had gone in, he would never reach the park – he would never come out of Nelly's the same. He won the battle – this time.

The walk in the park would clear his mind and allow him to focus and think through his issue with Forrest. He was searching for the trifecta. An angle that would first keep the peace with Chao; second help Forrest; and third give Paula the opportunity she needed. He found a bench overlooking the pond where little kids would race their sailboats. He sat there for a moment, thinking about the many times he had helped Cory launch his sailboats at this pond.

The air was downright cold – just forty-eight degrees. Steam was coming off the pond and the morning sun cut through the tall trees casting long, cool shadows. Johnson always thought that he could find this place blindfolded simply by following the familiar scent of those eucalyptus trees towering over the pond. This was his favorite place in the park. He came to sit and think, sometimes sitting there for hours.

As the sun began to warm the earth, an idea came to him. It was as if a great light had shinned down on him. Confident that his plan would work for everyone, he called his friend, Paula Chen.

Chapter 10

"Hey, Paula Chen. It's Mark Johnson. What's up with you stranger?" Johnson had known Paula Chen since high school and they remained good friends. Paula had introduced him to his wife, Chao-Xing. The three were close friends back then, much closer than they have been recently. Johnson and Chen had teamed up on the Farallones case earlier in the fall. Although she had been a great partner, Johnson was concerned about how she would feel about this call. Specifically, how would she react to becoming a Marin County investigator?

"Mark, it's great to hear your voice. I've been meaning to visit you one of these days but it's damn hard to find the time." So much for Johnson's fear about how she would react.

"How have you been, Paula? Tell me what's going on. I'd like to see you one of these days too."

"Well, there's not too much new with me, Mark. You know, it's the same old same old." The truth of the matter was that Chen's life was a total mess. She hesitated at first, but felt she could trust him with her news. "Mark, the brass decided that my move to Cyber Crimes will be permanent." With her voice quivering, she went on. "They said I'd never work the homicide desk again." For Chen, this was a difficult pill to swallow. One she did not take easily.

"That's stupid on so many levels, Paula. You're one of the best detectives I've ever worked with."

"I gotta' tell you, Mark. After I was shot two years ago, I had to work my ass off to get back the physical and mental acuity needed to perform the job at a high level. I was rock-hard and ready and they knew it. But it wasn't good enough for the guys at the top." Johnson could hear in her voice that Chen's spirit had been broken by the SFPD's decision. She had become consumed with self-pity. She stopped caring about her job – and herself too. Paula began leaving work early, or would simply call in sick, just to sit at home and wallow in her misery. Worst of all, she began to eat like a horse.

Chen was in a bad place. She would go for days at a time without ever leaving her house. She kept the window coverings down, which made the house dark and gloomy. Flies swarmed around the partially empty fast food containers strewn everywhere. Pizza boxes, piled high on the coffee table in front of the

TV, still had pieces of days-old pizza in them. Dirty dishes, stacked in the sink, were starting to smell. One of the neighbors stacked up her un-read newspapers, still in their orange plastic sleeves, like cordwood outside her door. Chen, who had been in excellent shape, gained fifteen pounds over the past five weeks.

"What are you going to do next, Paula?" asked Johnson. No answer.

Struggling to stay focused on the conversation with Johnson, Paula managed to ask, "How is your recovery going, Mark?"

"I'm fine. How about today, Paula?"

"What? What about today?" Chen dreaded the idea of Johnson seeing her like this. In no mood to face reality she said, "I...ah...I don't know, Mark."

"Maybe we could meet for lunch? I've got a proposal for you."

"Hell no, Johnson. The last time we met for lunch we ended up doing something we shouldn't have done. You almost got yourself killed and I almost got myself fired."

"Come on, Paula. Was it really all that bad?"

"Truth is, Mark. I think I really enjoyed it."

"You *think* you enjoyed it?"

"Fine, Mark. It was a great experience." After a brief moment of reflection she said, "And I also appreciated the confidence you showed in me on that case." She was referring to her role on a Bay Area task force involving the theft of nuclear waste from the waters off the Farallon Islands.

"Paula, I'm dead serious. I need to talk to you. You have to hear what I want to share with you. Trust me, Paula. I know you'll be interested in the proposal I have for you."

Chen began to spark up a little when she heard the word "proposal." Perhaps it would be the boost she needed. Reluctantly, Paula said, "Listen, it won't work; lunch I mean. How 'bout I come over to your house later today. Is three-thirty ok?"

"Sure. Sounds good, Paula. See you then."

* * *

Ever since he had been shot, Johnson's mother came to visit him nearly every day. She had a rather controlling personality, like many Italian mothers, and her daily visits had become, well, annoying to Johnson. Chao saw her walking toward the house. She put on a smile, waved and called out to her, "Hi, Sophia," hoping it would alert Johnson to her arrival.

"Ciao, Chao." Chao had learned to tolerate Sophia over the years. She was her Mother-in Law after all. Sophia was focused on something else today. "I want to speak with Mark. Where is he?"

"He's out back in the Tea Garden." Chao did greet her with a hug and an obligatory kiss on the cheek, "I'll walk you out there."

"No, no. That's fine, my dear, I'm sure I can find my way on my own."

Johnson knew that his mother wanted to talk to him about changing his career – again. Having tried a number of angles to convince him to get out of police work, he refused to allow the conversation to move in that direction. Johnson and his mother sat in the tea garden for the longest time before either one of them spoke – a true "Sicilian Standoff."

For weeks, Sophia had tried to convince her son to retire, or at least go into a less dangerous line of work. "Mark," she began, breaking the silence first, "I would be happy to give you whatever you need money-wise for you to start a new career. And of course, there's still a place for you in the family business too." The family business was importing olive oil from Sicily and selling it stateside. She had been pressuring Mark to manage the logistics department. Sophia, a wealthy woman, meant well and wanted the best for her son. Unfortunately, her endless droning about getting out of police work and into something else was driving him crazy.

"Mother, please. As I've told you before, when I decide to retire from police work, I'll retire for good. I appreciate your concerns, but for now, I've decided to go back to detective work."

"Dio mio, Marco. I'll kill myself if you do that," she said, laying on the guilt in a way that only an Italian mother can.

"Mother, please. If you kill yourself, you can not have a Church funeral." Johnson regretted insulting her. *I shouldn't have said that.*

Sophia's pride got the better of her. She stood up in a rage and slapped him hard, across his face. Johnson sat there in shock as she stormed back into the house.

Chao had seen her mother-in-law's many moods over the years but she had never seen her quite this angry. "Sophia, wait. What's wrong?" Chao asked.

"What's wrong?" She said it again, a little louder, "What's wrong? That pezzo-di-merda husband of yours is talking about going back to police work. I don't like the idea, Chao. I DO NOT LIKE IT." Sophia was out the door and into her Beamer. "Puttana," yelled Sophia as she drove away.

"Mark, what did you do to piss her off?"

"Chao, I told her I was thinking about going back to the Homicide Desk. Then she began to lay on the guilt. You know how she goes on."

"Mark, what in the hell are you talking about?"

"Chao, I know. I'm really confused."

"What about those nightmares? You need to get some counseling and get your head screwed on straight. Yesterday you said you didn't want to go back to the homicide desk, but today you do?"

"Believe me, Chao, I know you're right. Just hear me out, please. Forrest has been good to us during my time off. Right?"

"Yes, I know. He's been very supportive."

"He's really short handed and the bad guys, well, they don't take any days off."

"So what? That's his problem."

"I know. But one last case gives him some time to hire and train my replacement."

"He hasn't even tried to hire anyone in the past two months."

"True, he had expected me to come back. I'll make it clear that it's my last case. The other thing is that staying active until February gets me to twenty-five years with the county and enhanced benefits."

Chao just stood there looking up at him for the longest time. Her dark brown eyes began to swell with tears. Johnson was not quite sure what to do. He took her hands holding them in his. She couldn't stop herself from responding and reaching out to him. Finally, she spoke, "One more case, Mark?

Right. Come on, I'll believe *that* when I see it. I want to see the world *with you*. I want to grow old *with you*. I want to wake up *with you* lying next to me every morning. I want to raise our grandkids *with you*."

"Grandkids? Is one of the girls pregnant?"

"No. Not yet anyway," then she said, "I don't ever want to see you with tubes in your face again."

Desperate to change the subject, Johnson said, "Did you know that Paula's been reassigned *off of* the homicide desk – permanently?"

"No, I didn't. That's gotta' be tough..."

"I'm working on a plan in which Forrest hires her as a permanent member of the department. If he agrees to that, I would commit to coming back for one last case – but only if you are ok with it."

"Do you think he'll go for that, Mark?" Chao asked, starting to soften a little.

"Yes. Forrest saw her in action when she helped out on the last case. She impressed him."

"I bet she's really angry about being taken off the homicide desk. I'll give her a call. Maybe set up a girl's day out, you know, spa, hair, nails, etcetera."

"Good idea, Chao. She's coming over here at three thirty today. You can ask her about it then."

"Three thirty? Damn it, Mark, that was twenty minutes ago. You didn't leave me time to straighten up the house and change into something nice."

"For Christ's sake, Chao, it's Paula. No need to go off the deep end." Johnson glanced at his watch and noticed it was three fifty-eight. *Strange. Paula prides herself on being punctual. I hope she didn't get cold feet.* Ten minutes later there was a knock at the front door. When Johnson opened it, he couldn't believe what he saw.

Chapter 11

The weather had turned cool. In San Francisco, cool is anything below fifty-five degrees. Paula was dressed in loose fitting sweats and a heavy pea coat, the kind worn by sailors. It kept her warm plus it fit. Self-conscious about her added girth she used the pea coat as a cover-up too. "Mark, before you say a goddamn word, you need to understand where I've been."

"Ok, Paula. Fine. Please come in." She entered and Johnson greeted her with a welcomed embrace, the kind old friends share. The two had always been close but there had never been any romantic spark. "Lets go sit in the garden and talk."

Chao appeared from nowhere, and she too put her arms around Paula to give her support. "Paula, I want you to know that I'm here for you," she whispered in her ear. "In fact, Mark and I are both in your corner. Mark told me that you were deep sixed by those assholes in the city."

"Thanks, Chao. I'll get over it. It hurts, but I'm adjusting – slowly. I came over to borrow some of Mark's old clothes. You may not realize it but I've gained a few pounds," so typical of Paula to use humor to lighten a mood. Johnson didn't catch the joke but the two women shared a good laugh – laughter had been missing in both of their lives for far too long.

Mark took Paula's arm. "It's good to see you, my friend," he said as they walked to the garden. "Chao, you are welcome to join us if you want."

"No thanks. Not right now. I've got some stuff to finish up first. I'll be out in a minute with a couple blankets." Johnson and Paula walked to the garden. "I'll bring some tea shortly," she promised. "After all, that's why we call it a *tea* garden,"

The tea garden was Johnson's pride and joy. He had worked on it for most of the summer. It was a gift from him to Chao for their anniversary. Their house sat on an odd-shaped lot that backed up into a steep hill. The hill was covered with thick brush, vines of ivy, flowering cacti and hanging succulents.

The combination of natural rock and plants had inspired Johnson to build a Tea Garden. He dug a koi pond complete with a mini-replica of the arched bridge in the Japanese Tea Garden at Golden Gate Park. Colorful lanterns hung from overhead wires to light up the space. His favorite place was a secluded sitting area surrounded by a collection of bonsai trees and his prized California Polypody Ferns.

Johnson had rehearsed what he would say to Paula a hundred times. He knew what to say but wanted to make sure he said it in a way that would not offend her. Unfortunately, all of that prep work was for naught – he just blurted it out. "Paula, I've been thinking about going back to work. Chao is dead-set against it and I don't want to hurt her any more than I already have."

"Whoa, Mark. Slow down a bit, please. Tell me how you going back to work involves me? I'm not following."

"I want you to come be my partner and work with me in Marin." Silence can be deafening, and it sure was right then. Then Johnson went on, "Paula, you're an excellent detective. You have keen insights and a really strong grasp of procedure."

"But Mark, the SFPD pigeon-holed me. They don't think I'm physically or mentally able to do the job. How do I explain that away to Marin County?"

"The SFPD did it for liability reasons. Look, you got shot on their watch. Right? Putting you back in the field again, even though you're physically ready, leaves them with some liability and the potential for a huge law suit if you get hurt again."

"Why wouldn't it be the same in Marin?"

"As long as you pass the physical, you're good to go. Forrest told me to tell you that whenever you are ready he..."

"Thanks," she said cutting him off. "And please, thank Lieutenant Forrest for me. But tell him that I have to say no."

"Paula, why 'No'? Don't you want to get back into homicide again?" He was really miffed that she had the audacity to ruin his plan. Paula would love to get back into homicide again but the truth is that she did not want to work for Johnson. She had always admired his brilliance but there's no way she could put up with his arrogance on a daily basis.

She offered a rather weak excuse, "I couldn't do the commute everyday like you do. It's gotta' be at least a two hour round trip from my house."

"Paula, how long does it take you to get to your current office?"

"I take side streets and the drive to the Mission Bay station takes anywhere from twenty-five to thirty-five minutes each way from my house."

"I heard the Cyber unit is moving to a vacant building near the waterfront, closer to AT&T Park."

"Yeah, I know, but that's not much farther than the Mission Bay office and it won't add much time; but the parking really sucks."

"It only takes about thirty-five minutes to drive to San Rafael from the Sunset. The traffic flows into the city in the morning and flows out during for the afternoon rush. You'd be going counter-commute. So, working out of San Rafael won't add much time. That's not a good reason, Paula. Level with me..."

Paula knew Johnson had her. She couldn't bear to hurt him with her real concern...so she lied again. "Mark, it's always difficult whenever friends try to create a 'boss-subordinate' relationship. The baggage from their friendship always seems to get in the way." She saw the disappointment on his face but continued. "Mark, don't take this the wrong way but I'm not sure we could work together every day. We each have strong personalities and eventually they're going to clash."

"So what? Diversified points of view help solve cases. If two people agree on everything all the time, then one of them isn't needed. Our challenge would be to keep it from getting personal."

"I don't know," Paula was softening. "What about Chao? We've become close again and I don't want her to blame me in any way for you going back into homicide again."

"Chao will be able to deal with it. Let me share something that's highly confidential. I plan to tell Forrest that I'd work for him on two conditions.

94

The first one is that this will be my final case as a Marin County Sheriff's Detective."

"Right, Mark. Like you'll just walk away. There's nobody on the planet that will buy that one."

"Second," Johnson said, ignoring her response. "You'd be named as my replacement with the same grade, pay and responsibilities that I have. In fact, I'd work *for you* on this case. If Forrest will say yes to those two points, I'll come back. If not, I'm gone. It's that simple."

"Mark, are you back on the booze or is it the pain meds doing the talking?"

"Look Paula, it's the best way I can think of to please Chao, give Forrest the help he needs right now, and help you too."

"Would you really be able to step back and let me take the lead?" There was a brief silence before Johnson spoke again.

"Paula, there's something I haven't told you."

"What's that?"

"I'm suffering from PTSD since my shooting. I'm dealing with it but I wanted you to know about it. You may be getting stuck with a certified nut-job watching your back."

"Mark, you need to deal with this PTSD thing before you grab a weapon and go back in the field with me."

"I know."

"I don't want a fifty-one fifty as a partner."

"And I wouldn't either. But I'm not cray-cray, Paula. At least not yet."

"Oh boy. That's reassuring."

"With me, my issues are at night, in my dreams. I can't get that shooter out of my mind. Chao never knew I had a problem. Would you feel better if I didn't carry a weapon?"

"No, of course not. I would never say 'yes' to being your partner if I couldn't trust you, Mark. But this whole thing is so sudden. I'm way out of shape both physically and mentally. I need a little time to digest it all; maybe loose a few pounds too. And you, you need time to make sure you get your head on straight."

"Paula, take a few days to think about it, please. If you have any questions, or just want to talk more, please get back to me."

"Sure, Mark. Thanks for your confidence in me. It means a lot. Can I talk to Chao about this?"

"Give me a few days to go over the details with Forrest one more time. Regarding Chao, I haven't discussed it with her yet. I'll call you when it's ok to talk to her." As Johnson and Chen were wrapping up their conversation, Chao brought out a tray with a pot of freshly brewed tea and three cups. The three of them sat there visiting for a while, enjoying the moment, careful to avoid any talk of work.

When they had finished their tea, Johnson and Chao walked Paula to the front door. The two women hugged, said their goodbyes and vowed to get together more often, maybe even do lunch.

Chao reached her arm around Johnson's waste as they watched Paula walk to her car. "Mark, she was really down when she got here. But now, she's leaving with a much lighter mood. You must have given her hope." There's no denying that Paula was depressed and on the verge of doing something desperate. She had lost more than her job; she had lost her self-confidence and identity. The meeting with Johnson, however, gave her an emotional boost, a new pathway into her future. She would definitely consider the offer but she wasn't ready to commit to anything just yet.

"I'm not sure what more I can do for her. I pitched the idea of her coming to work with me as a Marin County homicide detective. She balked at it, said the commute was too long."

"That's bullshit, Mark. I know she has concerns about working *with* you on a permanent basis, and even more concern about working *for* you. When the two of us were sitting together in the ER after you got shot, she referred to you as the perfect FOUR."

The number four in the Chinese culture represents extremely bad luck. "In her mind you're cursed."

"Chao, I told her that the arson case would be my final case as a homicide detective. I told her that she would be the lead detective on the case and that I would essentially work for her."

"Mark, you're serious about hanging up your badge, aren't you? I don't want you to do that for me...I could never live with that guilt."

"No, Chao. I'm doing it for us. Plus," Johnson laughed, "The idea of sharing an apartment with Jonah is wrong on so many levels." Johnson was trying to inject a bit of humor into what had become a serious discussion. "Chao, listen, I can honestly say that I'm ready to move in a new direction. But it's only worth doing if you are willing to move there with me. Are you ok if I talk to Forrest about this idea? I really need some feedback from you. Please tell me what you are thinking?"

Chao smiled. "It's a good plan, Mark. I know we'll be able to make it work. Go ahead and run it by Lieutenant Forrest." Then, with a twinkle in her eye she said, "I don't think Cory will be home from school for at least forty-five minutes..."

Chapter 12

Paula couldn't stop thinking about the job offer Johnson had discussed with her. She had given up all hope of ever working the homicide desk again and was energized by their conversation.

Paula spent the next day cleaning her house. She collected and threw out all of the food containers; washed the dishes; and did three loads of laundry. The more she thought about Johnson's plan, the more angry she became at how the San Francisco Police Department had dumped her, eliminating her future. She knew that working for the Marin County Sheriff's office was an opportunity that could take her life in a new direction. *I don't want to miss out by waiting. I'm going to call him now.*

Excited and eager to cement the deal, she called Johnson, to make sure the plan that they had discussed was still on the table. "Mark Johnson, you are a great salesman. I've done nothing but think about your proposal ever since I left your house."

"Hey, Paula. What are you talking about?" He was toying with her of course...but she was not sure.

"I've been thinking about the job you and I had talked over; you know, me working for Lieutenant Forrest."

"Ah, Paula...I don't recall discussing exactly who you'd be working for."

"Mark, I remember you saying that you would actually work for me. Doesn't that mean that I'd be reporting to Forrest?"

"I did say that, Paula. But I'm starting to have some second thoughts on the reporting structure."

"Listen. Once you pluck your head from your ass and figure out what's what, please let me know."

"Paula, I'm just busting your balls. I'd be happy as your second, if you would have me."

"I don't have any balls to bust, or haven't you ever noticed?"

"Boy oh boy, you could have fooled me."

"Let's get down to it." Paula's voice took a serious tone. "I'm ready to accept the offer. I'd love to work on the Marin County homicide desk."

"Paula, are you serious? That's really great news. Welcome aboard."

"Thanks, Mark."

"We should find a time to meet with Forrest. Does next Monday or Tuesday work for you?"

"Either of those days is fine. Once you have the meeting details set up with Forrest, call me with the plan."

Johnson was ecstatic when he called Lieutenant Forrest with the news. "Denny, I've been talking to Paula Chen and came up with a plan that I know you're gonna like."

"Great, Mark. I'm listening."

"First off, Paula has agreed to make the switch and join the Marin County Homicide unit with the understanding that she would be my replacement."

"So far, so good, although, I was going to slot her into Bartlett's position as your new partner."

Johnson was thrown off at first when Forrest said he would use Chen to replace Bartlett. He went on, "Denny, Paula's experienced and should be paid the same as I'm getting paid. Right?"

"Ah, ok. Sure..." said a bewildered Forrest. It sounded like he was not heavily invested in what Johnson was pitching to him, but he continued to listen to what he was saying.

"I'll be happy to spend time showing her the ropes. I'll also make sure she gets up to speed with departmental procedures. Oh, and I want to work *for* her on the Tomales arson case rather than having her reporting to me. When the case is solved, I'll submit my official retirement papers."

"And?"

"And what, Denny?"

"And how do I sell this load-a-crap to *my* boss?"

"Denny, come on. What part of this do you take issue with?"

"Just the part about giving her your grade; the part about paying her what you're getting; the part about you working for her; and the part about you retiring when the arson case is solved." Forrest then said in a rather tongue-in-cheek way, "Other than those few points, everything else is just fine."

"Damn it, Denny, this is what we had discussed. What's changed? If she's my replacement, you really should pay her what I get paid. Right?"

"Sure, I guess, but I don't like the idea of her waltzing right in and being 'in charge', Mark. How will the guys react to that?"

"Denny, if you thought for one minute that any of 'the guys' you're talking about were capable of successfully filling my shoes, we wouldn't be having this conversation. We both know what the reality is, Denny – those guys aren't ready to lead yet."

"Mark, I don't know. I'm just not comfortable putting her in charge."

"It's better for you, Denny, and for her. It will give you continuity, plus she's more stable than I am right now. I hate to say this, but I think the real concern you have is that *I'm* leaving. I don't think you can accept that." There was silence on the other end. Johnson remembered what his mother had taught him about negotiating – state your position and then shut up. She would tell him over and over again, *"Mark, remember; the next one to talk loses."* Johnson didn't say a word as he waited for Forrest to say something. After what felt like an eternity, he finally got a response from Forrest.

"Alright, I'm ok with everything except her salary. I don't have the budget for that." It was the rainy season in the Bay Area and a heavy band of showers was moving through the Sunset District. It was loud, making it hard to hear. Rain was coursing down the streets. Johnson grew concerned watching the water collect in his tea garden. Those terra cotta pots weren't draining fast enough, his bonsai trees were flooding. Johnson had to raise his voice in order to speak over the sounds of the rain.

"That's a reasonable concern, Denny, it really is. Maybe you could cut my salary and give it to her. I'm fine with that if it makes the numbers work." Johnson shut up again. He waited for Forrest's response, anxiously wanting to run out to the garden and rescue his prized plants.

"Well...OK. Mark, I think I can make that work, at least on paper."

"That's great, Denny. Do you want to call her with the official offer?"

"She needs to fill out an application first. HR is sticky on that one. She should come up and fill out the application, then we can meet to talk details."

"How about next Monday afternoon. Does one o'clock work for you?"

"Let me check my calendar, just a minute...OK, Monday is good but two works better for me. Does that time work for you?"

"That's good. We'll see you at two o'clock in your office." Johnson called Chen to give her the news. "Paula. You're in. Congratulations. We meet with Forrest on Monday afternoon at two but there are a couple of formalities first, like filling out a job application. Lets do the HR stuff first and then we'll meet with him. Oh, we should set up a time to talk to the fire investigator, and Jonah, of course, too. We can review the evidence that's been collected so far in the Tomales case."

"Thanks, Mark. I'm anxious to get back to doing what I love. Once I get the offer from Forrest, I'll call the SFPD to let them know I'm done."

"What time should I pick you up or do you want to drive the two of us up to Headquarters?"

"I was thinking that I'd take my car so I can get a feel for the area. I want to look for an apartment close to Headquarters. Let's just meet at HQ." As soon as Paula hung up, Johnson called Chiang and Dibdall to see if they could meet at three o'clock on Monday to review the Tomales arson case.

* * *

"Paula, it's great to see you again. How have you been? Say, I never got the chance to thank you for the role you played in the Farallones Case."

"I've been well, Lieutenant. But I'll level with you, sir. The San Francisco PD has sidelined me. They took me out of homicide permanently."

"Yes, I'm aware of that and I'm aware of the incident in which you were injured. But let me ask you this, Paula. May I call you, Paula?"

"Please do."

"Are you able to pass a physical?"

"Yes. I can."

"That's good enough for me, Paula. SFPD's loss is our gain. Welcome aboard."

"Thanks, Lieutenant. I won't disappoint you."

* * *

"Let me make the introductions," said Johnson to the group that had assembled in the squad room.

"I want ya'll to meet Paula Chen. Some of you may already know her. She's joining the Marin County Sheriff's department and will be the lead investigator on the Tomales Arson case." In addition to Chiang, Dibdall, and Jurek, Johnson had invited Detectives Knox and Schmitz to meet Paula. They had been on Johnson's team for years and looked at each other in amazement. They weren't expecting that news.

"Welcome aboard, Paula. It's good to see you," said Dr. Chiang. Paula Chen, Johnson and Jonah Chiang had known each other for years.

"Hi, Paula. I'm Billy Dibdall, the Fire Marshal for Marin County. The situation is hot in Tomales right now and getting hotter. Those fires have been a real nut buster for us."

"I'm Jurek Grotowski, Miss Chen. Glad to meet you." Jurek was anxious to get started on the case. "I walked the scene and collected evidence at two of the fires – each of the ones that claimed a life. I work for Captain Dibdall."

"You all know me," said Johnson. "I've worked with Paula in the past. There's no one better to fill the void we have on the homicide desk. Let's get started." Johnson was at the whiteboard, marker in hand. "So what do we know about the victims?"

"Emily Donegras, eighty-two, found dead in bed at that first fire, on West Street," said Dr. Chiang.

"What do we know about her?" asked Johnson. "Come on, anything?"

"Well, sir..."

"Stop right there, Jurek. You're part of this team so call me Johnson, Mark, or shithead...but not sir."

"Sure, Mark," he said. "I had assumed that Miss Donegras died trying to escape the fire through the rear door of the house. However, even though the door had been jammed with a shovel, Doctor Chiang's report said she died from natural causes."

"That's true," said Chiang. "After I read Rollin's investigation notes I didn't see any reason to assume foul play. The body was found in bed. The autopsy showed neither pulmonary congestion nor edema caused by inhaling smoke. She died from a heart attack, not the fire. Initial ruling was that the fire didn't kill her directly...perhaps the fire caused the heart attack, but who knows? Jurek asked us to visit the Donegras fire after the fact and we did."

"When I went to investigate the Donegras fire I found a shovel, similar to the one at the Loomis fire, on the ground outside the back door."

"Was it jamming the door?" asked Johnson.

"No, I think it fell over. There were marks in the ground, which indicated that the shovel could have been used to jam the door. I found evidence of a burn trailer as well."

"Interesting," said Chen. "Jurek, can you sketch the layout of the scene for us on the whiteboard?"

"Sure, I've got the details for both fires. I'll draw the layout of scene at the Donegras fire first."

"Thanks, Jurek," After he drew the layout, Chen asked, "Where was her body found?"

Chiang jumped in, "My people were sent to the scene. Her body was still in bed when they found her. After recovering the remains, they took her to the lab for an autopsy. Standard procedure."

Jurek began drawing the layout of the Loomis fire. "You can see the relationship between where the fire started, where the woman had been sleeping, and the path she traveled to get to the rear door." The Loomis fire was Jurek's investigation and he was proud of the work he had done on it. He had drawn out the entire scene from his detailed investigation notes.

"You're thorough, Jurek." said Chen.

"Guys," said Johnson. "We need to stay focused on the first fire for now. What else do we know about the victim, ah...Miss Donegras?" Silence filled the room. "There are a number of knowledge gaps we need to address."

"Mark, the trail's getting cold. Maybe we should split up to get it done faster. You do the background on the first victim, and I'll focus on the second one,

Grace Loomis." After Paula offered her suggestion the mood in the room changed in an instant. *What's going on? Had she really taken over?* The good old boys of the Marin County Sheriff's office were stunned.

Johnson could feel a chill take over the room. "Good idea, Paula. Guys, like I said earlier, Paula's leading this investigation. I'm still recovering from my injuries." It was hard for Johnson to give up the lead but he had to reinforce the fact that Paula was in charge in order for her to receive the support and cooperation she would need.

Paula listed a litany of questions on the white board; "What do we know about their pasts? Were they married or single? Did they have kids? Where did they work? When did they retire? What's their financial situation? Do they have common friends?" Paula knew that these questions would lead to more. Eventually, these questions would begin to paint a picture of each victim and lead to a list of people who may have had the opportunity or the motive.

"Got it, Paula." Johnson said tersely, regretting the fact that she was in charge. "Let's see what we can learn about the victims and compare notes. Is there anything else we need from Billy and Jurek?"

"Yes, were the deaths related?" she asked.

"Jurek," said Dibdall, "You're most familiar with the details. Can you address that question?"

"Sure, Cap. For starters, we know that both of these women were advanced in age and both fires were two-stage fires. The victim in the first fire may have died from a heart attack, but we know for sure the victim in the second fire died trying to escape. She might have made it to safety but a shovel had jammed in the rear door, keeping her inside. Like I said, I found a similar shovel at the first fire along with evidence suggesting that it too may have been positioned to jam the rear door."

"I read your reports, Jurek. They were thorough and left me with the feeling that this is the work of a lone serial arsonist; a damn good one at that."

"Thanks, Ms. Chen...I mean, Paula. Here's my card in case you have any questions for me." Jurek left the meeting with Dibdall at four-thirty. Poking his head back into the room, Jurek said, "Oh, and one other thing, Paula. I learned that all three of the burned structures were owned by the same person."

After the others left, Paula stayed for a while longer. She thought about what Jurek had just told her. It had to be more than a coincidence that the same person owned all three buildings.

Chapter 13

Paula sat in silence in Johnson's office absorbing the essence of what was to become her office. Ever the pragmatist, she began making a list of a few changes she would make. At the top of the list was removing the gaudy picture of a ballerina that hung behind Johnson's desk. It was a two-bit copy of an Edgar Degas painting. She also counted six ashtrays. *What the hell? No one can smoke in California anymore. Why keep these?* Next on the list was the old leather couch. It looked comfortable but worn and likely infested with some sort of native wildlife; it too had to go. The blotter/calendar on Johnson's desk was seven years out of date. *My God...*

Paula would make these changes at some point, but not right now. Johnson was her friend, a friend who had gone the extra mile to help her get back into police work. Out of respect for him, she decided to leave the office the way it was. After all, it had been *his* for years. Paula knew she would make the changes in time but for now her focus had to be learning Marin County procedures and getting up to speed on the Tomales arson investigation.

* * *

Anxious to get started on the case, Paula drove to Tomales early the next morning to learn what she could about the fire and its victim, Grace Loomis. She took Highway One into town arriving at eight thirty in the morning. A property management office was on her right, Fieler's Property Associates. *I'll come back to talk to them when it opens at nine.*

She drove to the scene of the fire that claimed the life of Loomis. The house was badly charred, with nearly every window broken. It still had a band of yellow police tape wrapped around it to keep gawkers out. Paula walked into the backyard and there, exactly as Jurek had described it, she found the shovel. An eerie chill traveled down her spine the moment she saw it. It was still in place, still jamming the door shut.

Paula replayed in her mind what Jurek had told her about the similarity of the two fires. But the thing that was most important was the news that the same person owned all three houses. *This has to be more than a coincidence.*

Hot! In Tomales

Paula waited until it was a few minutes after nine. Anxious to learn more about the owner of the three houses, she walked into the property office and introduced herself to the young blond sitting at the reception desk. "I'm Detective Paula Chen with the Marin County Sheriff's Office. I would like to speak to whoever is in charge here."

"Sure," said the receptionist, who looked all of eighteen. "That would be Danny Fieler. I'm afraid he's indisposed right now, if you know what I mean. I'd be happy to tell him you wanna' talk to him as soon as he becomes available."

"That's fine. Thanks."

"Danny," the blond yelled to the back room, "There's someone here for you. A cop I think."

"I'll be right out," was his reply. A few minutes later, Danny Fieler walked to the front office drying his hands. Paula was going to shake his hand but quickly decided against it.

"Mr. Fieler, I'm Detective Chen. I'm in town to investigate the recent fires here in Tomales. I hope you can help shed some light on them for me."

"Sure thing, Detective. I'll help all I can."

"So, my understanding is that all three of the burned houses were owned by the same person."

"Well, sorta," replied Danny. "They're owned by the same legal entity, the La Ostra, LLC."

"Thanks, Mister Fieler. These days it seems as if half of California's owned by one LLC or another." Paula pronounced his name "filer" – like what a file clerk does. "What can you tell me about this La Ostra, LLC?"

"Not much," replied Danny. "And, by the way, my family pronounces our name "feeler", like those long whiskers on a shrimp or a cat."

"Sorry about that, Mister Fieler. Please go on."

"The articles of organization for LLC's are not open to the public but I do have a mailing address for them. They're in Eureka, on Humboldt Bay."

"Interesting," said Chen, "Eureka's a seven hour drive north of here, isn't it?"

"About five on the 101," Danny quickly replied.

"Do your records indicate *when* they purchased these houses?"

"Sure, Detective. But it'll take me a few minutes to find that. Please, take a seat if you want. I'll be back shortly." Paula looked around the tiny office and noticed a number of pamphlets sitting on the long oak table across from the receptionist. The one that caught her eye featured the San Andreas Fault. She read that it's the longest earthquake fault line in California. It starts in Eureka and extends south for seven hundred and fifty miles to San Diego. It runs right through the center of Tomales Bay, not far from where she was standing. *Why would anyone choose to live this close to an earthquake zone?*

"Detective Chen, I found some information for you." Paula went over to the counter where Fieler was standing. "The LLC purchased these properties over the past three months," he said. "One property was bought from Emily Donegras and the other two from Grace Loomis. They paid cash for all three."

"Grace Loomis owned two of them? Hmmm – did she rent out one of them?"

"Yes, I guess..." said Fieler. "The terms in the purchase agreement allowed for each of the women to stay in their houses for as long as they wanted. Of course they had to be able to physically take care of them and pay the rent on time."

"Do you know if any construction projects were planned that might have involved the land those properties sat on?"

"No. Nothing I'm aware of."

"Can you tell me if the LLC owns other land or properties in the area?"

"I didn't see any other local properties in their file. However, they do have some rather vast land holdings up north, in Humboldt County."

"Were they planning any more purchases?"

"Sorry, but we don't learn about a transaction until the purchase has been filed with the county.

115

We don't have any way of knowing ahead of time if a property is involved in active negotiations. Unless, of course, it involves one of the clients we represent – I'm also a real estate agent. I can tell you that none of my clients are working with that LLC."

"Thank you, Mister Fieler. You've been helpful. Here is my card. Please call me if you think of any other information that might be useful. Do you know what time the General Store opens?"

"They open every morning at six."

Paula figured that the General Store would be a good place to interview locals. As she walked in, the ambiance of the dimly lit store transported her back in time. As a child of six or seven she went to stores like this with her dad. Rows and rows of shelves were stocked with various types of canned goods. Dried items such as sugar and flour filled the room. Ropes and tools hung along the walls while other items, such as coon and rodent traps, hung from the rafters. Dusty and dated, the store smelled like an old attic that had been closed up for years.

A more pleasant aroma from a freshly brewed pot of coffee found Paula's senses. She followed her nose and found the pot of coffee, always at the ready, on the front counter. She poured herself a cup of rich dark coffee. It needed two packets of sugar and a large slug of milk to get the taste to her liking. An old-time cash register sat on the counter next to the pot. Its large keys had to be pushed down to ring up a sale. Not seeing a clerk, Paula put three dollars into the worn wicker basket that sat next to it. *That ought to cover the cost of the coffee.*

"Can I help you, Ma'am?" asked the elderly lady arranging laundry detergents. Paula was startled, not noticing her when she first walked in. Her nametag read "Harry," short for Harriet Grant.

"Harry, I'm Detective Paula Chen with the SF, I ah...I mean, the Marin County Sheriff's office," it would take Paula a little time to get used to her new title. "I would like to ask you about Grace Loomis. Did you happen to know her?"

"Course' I knew her – everyone knew her," she said with a heavy cough. "That poor woman *died* an awful death being burnt up an' all. That poor girl *lived* an awful life too."

"What do you mean she 'lived an awful life'?"

"Well, I was born right here in Tomales and been livin' here for goin' on seventy years now. I've known Gracie for most of them years. Fact is I rented a house from her for years. But I moved into the back of the store about two months ago."

"Back in the day, before slowing down some, Gracie was known as the town hottie," Harriet coughed again, a heavy phlegmy cough this time.

117

"What do you mean by, 'the town hottie'?"

"Well," Harry whispered, "Gracie was, uh...you know, hot to trot. She was the town whore and every guy around these parts knew her. She'd bed any man who bought her a drink at the saloon."

"Saloon? Where's that Harry? I didn't see it on the way into town."

"The saloon's gone, dear. It's the Tomales Café and Deli now. Gracie was a regular at the saloon. She'd stop in after her shift a shuckin' them oysters and knock back a couple of shots. Then she'd wash 'em down with a beer or two."

"Shucking oysters?" Chen did not know about the oyster business along Tomales Bay. It began in the nineteen forties and grew exponentially.

"Them oysters was a big business back in the day. Local folks worked in the grow-out facilities."

"Grow-out?"

"The water in Tomales Bay is perfect oyster water, cold and clean. The company grows 'em on racks out in the water. We call 'em grow out beds."

"So they get picked every so often?"

"Its called harvestin'. Then they're shipped live or they get shucked for the canners."

"What else do you remember about Loomis?"

"Well, one night, she got into it with a midget."

"Don't you mean a dwarf? A little person?"

118

"Whatever. The skinny was that this little 'dwarf' fella was 'sposed to be hung like a horse. At least that was the story them other girls told." A sly smile formed on Harry's face, "Never did see for myself now," her cough was heavier.

"Do you recall his name? The dwarf I mean?"

"I'm blankin' on the name right now. It'll come to me in a minute. That little fella drove truck for the oyster factory. But he's so short, he needed to have blocks taped onto the gas and break pedals."

"What was the name of the oyster factory?"

"The Dream Bay Oyster Company."

"Dream Bay, huh? Where's it located?"

"It used to be a few miles south along Tomales Bay. The Feds came in and shut them down almost two years ago. Put 'em clean outa' business."

"Do you know why they were shut down?"

"No idea, Hun. But, getting back to Gracie, one night there was this big commotion goin' behind the shuckin house. We found Gracie and that damned dwarf goin' at it on a pile of empty oyster shells."

"Fighting?"

"No, ma'am. They was a he'in and she'in ya' know. Well, they kept at it all summer long," Harry said with a little laugh and a lot more coughing. "Finally, that little shit, Perry, knocked her up. Perry. That was his name. Perry, ahh...Perry Sciandero."

"So they were a couple? Did they get married?"

"Naw. He was a long haul driver; went up the coast as far as Portland. He'd be gone a few nights at a time. He liked sowing them short little seeds a' his up and down the coast."

"Sounds like Perry didn't want to settle down."

"No shit. And like I told ya', Gracie would take in any guy she could. Story around these parts was she should a' had a revolving door put in her house to make it easier for all them guys to come and go."

"So, did she abort the baby?"

"Nope. She kept it. She used that baby as a meal ticket for years. She got a lot of money from the county to help her raise that boy," Harry reached for her cough syrup. "This cough's getting' worse."

"How did she know it was Perry's? I mean with all the guys she slept with..."

"I guess she assumed that, since he was the only little man in these parts, that it was his."

"Her baby was a dwarf too? Do you happen to remember what she named it?"

"Gracie named him Jimmy, after that cartoon bug, Jimmy-the-Cricket. The kid never had a chance with gettin' raised up in her home an' all."

"Did you know Jimmy very well? Can you recall the names of any of his friends? Do you know where he's living now?"

"Gracie would drag Jimmy into the shuckin' room and sit him in the corner while she worked. She couldn't afford to pay for someone to watch after him. I worked the same shifts as Gracie and got to know little Jimmy pretty good. He was on his own by the time he was twelve. That's when the county took him out a' Gracie's home."

"The county took her son from her?"

"She had a habit of taken guys in, like I said, and poor little Jimmy had to listen to his mom getting' it, damn near every night, from the next room. Can you imagine that? That kid never had a chance."

"No. I can't imagine what that poor child went through. Who called Child Protective Services?"

"No idea, Detective. They just showed up one day and took Jimmy away," Harry was coughing more as she told the story. The cough syrup wasn't helping her at all.

"Any idea where Jimmy's living today?"

"Not sure. But I remember hearing that Jimmy had eventually gone on to college and had himself a good job working for the state."

"Thanks, Harry. You've been helpful. Is there anyone else around that knows Grace or Jimmy?"

"Well, you could try talk'n to Angus McGee, that is if you can find him. He's kinda' slow to the trigger, if you know what I mean? Angus is Jimmy's cousin, a tall kid. He and Jimmy made an odd looking pair, easy to spot em' from a distance. Folks would say, 'here comes the long and short of it.' Those two, they was always together."

"Any idea where I might find Angus?"

"Angus works on his family's mule farm. It's out on Messerschmitt Road, about two miles from here. I don't see Angus much anymore; the family keeps him close to the farm. But a few weeks back Angus comes into the store, doesn't say hi or anything else. Then, outa' the blue, he puts a ten-spot on the counter and asks if he can get four containers of kerosene. Nothing else, just the kerosene."

Chapter 14

"Hey, Mark. It's Paula. I've got some interesting news on the arson case."

"Mornin', Paula. What'ya got?"

"I've spent the past few hours over in Tomales interviewing a few locals. That place is kind of like, well you know, a forgotten little world; it's like stepping back in time. The woman that runs the General Store, her name is Harry, gave me an earful about Grace Loomis."

"You're talking about the Loomis woman killed in the latest fire? Right?"

"Yes. Apparently Grace Loomis had a child out of wedlock when she was in her forties. She was the town whore, entertaining every guy she could in her bed. One of em' slipped one passed the goalie."

"You sayin' the child was the town whore?"

"No, Grace. It turns out she got pregnant by the local little guy; a truck driver for an oyster company. He goes by the name of Perry Sciandero. Grace's kid was a boy named, Jimmy. He was also a little person. He grew up in an awful environment."

"Whoa, Paula. You're going way too fast. Tell me about the oysters and the awful environment."

"He was exposed to things that most children are never exposed to, raised by a drunken whore of a mother. Eventually the county came in and took Jimmy away from her."

"Are you thinking that Jimmy might be one of our suspects? Do you think he killed his mother?"

"I don't know, I haven't had enough time to digest all of this. But get this; Jimmy grew up close to his cousin, Angus McGee. The two hung around together – they were inseparable. What's interesting is that about two weeks ago McGee bought four containers of kerosene at the local general store."

"Wow. That's big, Paula. Kerosene was the key accelerant discovered at the scene of the fire. Are you ready to bring them in?"

"No. Not yet. We need to do more digging on Jimmy Loomis first. I have a work address for him over in San Rafael. I'm almost there now."

"Sounds good. Let's go over our notes back at the office. I'll be there about noon."

"It's almost ten right now, twelve-thirty or so might be better. Were you able to learn anything about the first victim, Ms. Donegras, yet?"

"Not much. I did learn that she worked at one of the oyster grow-outs along Tomales Bay."

"Was it The Dream Bay Oyster Company?"

"Sure was, Paula. How in the hell did you know that? She retired about fifteen years ago."

"Looks like a connection, Mark. I learned that Grace Loomis worked at Dream Bay and I believe she retired a few years ago as well."

"The victims knew each other. Do you think someone may have had a work-related reason to target those two women?"

"That's a good question, Mark. Gotta go. I'm about to walk into the office where Jimmy Loomis worked. I'll call you when I'm done and fill you in on what I learned here."

* * *

Paula arrived at the California Department of Transportation offices, Jimmy's last known work address. The massive building looked cold with dark terrazzo floors, gray marble walls, and heavily tinted glass. The receptionist, sitting at a desk in the lobby, was engrossed in her copy of People Magazine. She didn't notice Paula walk in. Paula approached her, cleared her throat to get her attention and said, "Good morning. I'm Detective Chen with the Marin

County Sheriff's Office. I would like to speak to the head of your HR department."

"Sure thing, Ma'am. HR is on third floor. Just take the elevator to three and turn to your left."

Paula pushed the up button and fidgeted a bit as she waited for the elevator. She couldn't help but wonder why the state would keep such a worthless position filled. *That girl could be replaced by a building directory sign.* When the elevator door opened Paula wondered if there would be an elevator operator manning it... *This state can think of more ways to waste money...no wonder we're bankrupt.* The car arrived and the large brass door opened for her – on it's own. The paneling inside the elevator was dark mahogany with an array of mirrors, set in polished brass frames. The mirrors began at about waist high and went all the way up to the ceiling. Paula pushed 'three' and the doors closed slowly.

Approaching the HR offices Paula stopped at another receptionist. "Good morning. I'm Detective Chen with the Marin County Sheriff's Department. I'd like to speak to the head of HR."

"Yes, Ma'am. The receptionist in the lobby called to let me know who you are and why you're here. Can I see your badge please?" Paula, surprised that the girl in the lobby had gotten her nose out of her magazine long enough to contact this clerk, was miffed by all the red tape. *It's easier to see the Governor.* Reluctantly, she pulled out her badge and showed it to her. "Thanks, Ma'am. I'll see if Miss Bridges has time to see you. Please take a seat."

Fifteen minutes turned into twenty. Finally the clerk walked over to where Paula was sitting. "She can see you now, Detective Chen. If you'll follow me I'll take you to her."

Paula was escorted into a small meeting room and introduced to Markella Bridges, the head of HR for California's Department of Transportation. In the room with Bridges was, Katherine Goldfarb. Goldfarb was the IT Supervisor who had managed the group in which Jimmy Loomis worked. Chen introduced herself to both women.

"Let me start," said Goldfarb. "I was the direct supervisor of Mister Loomis for four plus years. He was a genius, especially in the technology supporting our IT programs. But, Mister Loomis had a difficult time meshing with society."

"How so?" Chen asked.

"He seemed to hate everyone around him. This was especially true with women and most, well, all minorities. What's worse, he had zero patience for people with disabilities, which I thought strange."

"Because he's a dwarf himself? Or do you think there's another reason?"

"No, I think it's because he's a dwarf. He hates the fact that he's a little person."

"Katherine," said Bridges, "could you please take a minute and explain to Miss Chen the specific actions leading to the dismissal of Jimmy Loomis?"

"Sure, Markella. Mister Loomis worked here at Cal-DOT for six and a half years. Most of that time he was a systems programmer. Like I said, he was bright. He led a few projects, and overall, did a good job. However, most people kept their distance from him. A chronic complainer, he had something bad to say about everything and everybody."

"So, did you fire Loomis because he complained too much?" Chen asked.

"No. I fired him because he became abusive to the people he worked with. We tried to coach him. HR even helped us set up a special program for him in hopes of correcting his behavior. We also tried to keep him away from the staff by offering an early morning start-time of five-thirty. We hoped it would keep him away from the others. That was when he became abusive with me."

"Physically? Verbally? What did he do, exactly?" asked Chen.

"Not physically so much, but verbally," replied Goldfarb. "His language was awful, cursing all the time. He called the women he worked *with*, and *me*

128

too, 'stupid bitches' or 'dumb whores' and would often referred to us using the 'C' word. He was the most abrasive individual I had ever known."

"Did the women he offended complain directly to you?" Chen asked. "Or go straight to the HR?"

"They complained directly to me at first and I asked him a number of times to cool it. When that didn't work, we approached HR together."

"So he didn't like women?" asked Chen. *I can understand why that is.*

"Loomis didn't reserve his crass behavior just for women. We use a large contingent of contract resources from India in IT. Loomis would refer to them as 'Dot Heads' or 'Rag-Tops' and ask over and over, to the point of exhaustion, if their bindis, you know, those red dots on their foreheads, were reset buttons. He kept it up. It was very disturbing and I had to do something"

"How did Loomis react to the complaints from his co-workers? More importantly, how did he react to his dismissal?"

"He got angry. I called security to escort him out. He said he had a handgun at home and he knew how to use it. He vowed to come back here and 'settle the score' with everyone...especially me."

"Did he ever come back in with his gun?" Chen asked.

"Detective Chen," said Bridges, "We take these threats very seriously. We placed our lobby security on alert and added an armed guard in case Loomis ever did come back. Fortunately, he never did."

"I know this sounds like a dumb question, but did Loomis have any close friends?" asked Chen.

"People with Jimmy's personality generally don't have friends. They're angry all the time and that personal anger pushes people away," said Goldfarb. "He was highly toxic and just plain anti-social."

"Was he ever sexually abusive?" Chen asked.

"Interesting you should ask. Loomis did a lot of boasting about his sexual exploits with women. But he never got close to any of the women he worked with. He liked to brag about the size of what he called his 'joy stick'. Nobody here ever saw it or at least didn't admit to seeing it. He bragged that he could pick up any girl he wanted at the local bars. No one believed him until one day he brought in an attractive young woman into the office with him."

"Do you remember her name?" Chen asked.

"Yes, I do. Her name is Lorraine Cordiva," said Bridges. "I remember it because he asked me to add her as a beneficiary on his life insurance policy."

"Do you have an address for Miss Cordiva?"

"Yes, Detective, right here in his file. It's the address and phone number she gave us when she filled out the beneficiary forms." Bridges wrote it down for Paula.

"Oh, I see it's spelled with an 'e'." Chen thanked the women for their time and took the information for Cordiva. She headed back to headquarters to meet with Johnson to compare notes.

* * *

"Hey, Paula," said Johnson as he sat at his desk, the one with the awful ballerina picture hanging behind it, "Would ya' mind a whole lot if I took her with me?"

"Take who?"

"My ballerina. She's been standing right behind me for years."

My lucky day, but Poor Chao, she will have to look at it now. "Mark, please I want you to have it. It means a lot to you, I know. I'll find something else to put in her place." *A blank wall would be an improvement.*

"So what did you learn this morning? Go ahead and use the white-board if you want," said Johnson.

"For starters, our victims worked together in the shucking room at the Dream Bay Oyster factory." Paula wrote it on the white board. "Grace was the town whore and got pregnant by a dwarf. Her son, Jimmy Loomis, is also a dwarf."

"Emily Donegras, on the other hand, was the town prude," added Johnson. "Never drank, never had a boyfriend, nothin'. She was the type of person that waited for the light to say 'walk' before she'd use the crosswalk."

"Mark, Tomales doesn't have crosswalks."

"It was an illustratorial comment, Paula."

"Not sure if that's a word, Mark, but go on."

"There were no obvious reasons for anybody to hate or harm Miss Donegras. I can't find a single motive."

"Mark, here's the rest of what I learned. First, all three of the torched buildings were owned by the same entity. It's called the La Ostra, LLC and their home office is up in Eureka."

"Hmmm, what else does that LLC own?"

"Around here just the three houses in Tomales but they have other holdings in Eureka. The LLC paid these women cash for their houses. Oh, and Grace Loomis owned two of the buildings."

"Why would the LLC pay cash? It makes no sense unless they were trying to hide the purchase."

"I agree. We need to dig a little deeper on the LLC, Mark. The other thing I learned from Harry, the clerk at Tomales' General Store, is how Grace Loomis raised Jimmy. The poor kid grew up in an awful environment. She would pick up guys at the bar, take them home with her and 'pleasure' them while her son listened from the next room."

"That probably screwed him up a lot."

"Jeez, Mark. Ya' think? Jimmy was fired from Cal-DOT a few weeks ago because he was abusive to his co-workers. Here's the strange part; at the time he got fired, he had a steady girlfriend named Lorraine Cordiva. I've got her address and phone."

"Jimmy certainly had a motive for wanting to kill his mother, but you said that his friend, Angus McGee, bought the kerosene. What the hell...?"

"Mark, Angus is Jimmy's cousin. The two of them grew up together in the Tomales area. I think it's time to talk to them."

"I agree. I'll follow up with Jimmy and Cordiva. Would you mind driving back to Tomales to interview McGee?"

"That's fine." She was dreading the drive back to Tomales. It's a long, tedious drive due to all of the meandering twists and turns in the road. "See you later, Mark."

"We need to make sure to include Jurek in the discussion. After all, not only is it his investigation, he can help us with the technical aspects of an arson investigation.

Chapter 15

"James Loomis," yelled Johnson as he pounded on the door. "Open up right now. Marin County Sheriff, Jimmy. Open the door..." Johnson realized that nobody was in the apartment. Without a search warrant he had no choice but to leave. Walking back to his car, he saw someone crouching behind a car in the parking lot. *That's a damn dwarf.* Johnson yelled out to him, "Police. Stop right there. Turn around." The little person took off running, dodging cars in the parking lot. *Why is that little shit running?* Johnson was out of shape because of his surgery. It was an effort for him to run, but because his legs were twice as long as Jimmy's, he was able to catch him and pin him down across the hood of a late-model blue Buick. Panting and out of breath, Johnson asked, "Are you Jimmy Loomis?"

"Hey. What do you want, man?" Replied the dwarf, squirming to get free; never acknowledging that he was, in fact, Jimmy Loomis.

Hot! In Tomales

"I'm Detective Johnson with the Marin County Sheriff's Office." Johnson pulled his wallet out of a coat pocket to display his badge. The badge had a dent in it, it saved his life by stopping the fatal bullet when he was shot two months ago. "Show me some I.D. fella. We need to have a chat about the recent fires out in Tomales."

"Detective, I don't have any idea what you're talkin' about." Jimmy slowly removed his driver's license from his wallet and handed it over.

Johnson figured that Jimmy's motive to start the fires was revenge – revenge for the way his mother abused him during his childhood. "Listen, Loomis. Your mother, Grace Loomis, was murdered in one of those fires a few weeks back."

"Are you kidding me man? That old bat is finally dead? I couldn't care less. But listen, someone else gets the credit for it, Detective. Not me."

"Jimmy, you really carry a deep hatred for your mother, don't you?" Johnson said this with his hand firmly on Jimmy's throat. "You grew up in Tomales, you know the area, and you stand to inherit a lot of money from her estate. These things make you a prime suspect. Tell me where you were and what you were doing the evening of December first?"

"That's easy, Detective. I was in Chicago with my girl, Lorraine Cordiva. Go ahead, ask her."

"Why were you in Chicago? It's pretty cold there in December, isn't it?"

"Sure is. We stayed for a week after celebrating Thanksgiving with some old friends; friends I made during my 'Dwarf Tossing' days."

"Dwarf Tossing?" Johnson asked, not believing a word Jimmy was saying to him.

"Yeah, at O'Grady's Bar in Chicago. They were one of the first bars in the States to feature it. I had left home a few months before, with my cousin, Angus. We funded our adventure by doing odd jobs across the country. Our money finally ran out in Chicago, and we were desperate. O'Grady's was just getting into this 'Dwarf Tossing' event that the Aussies had started."

"You're full a' shit, Jimmy. Let's go."

"No man. I'm serious. Teams of two people, one being a dwarf of course, would compete to see how far they could toss the little person. The team that won got forty bucks, twenty each."

"Bullshit, Jimmy. I don't believe a word you're telling me. How could the city allow that? I would think the liability issue alone would be huge – doesn't the dwarf get banged up on the landing?"

"No. They had set up inflatable cushions for us to land on, like the kind they use in movie stunts. Angus was able to toss me nearly twelve feet."

"When did this take place?"

"Let me think. It must have been back in the late eighties. I was in my teens, eighteen or nineteen. Angus and I did pretty well. We held the Chicago record for a while...that is until City Hall decided to shut it all down."

"Tell me what you did when the city shut down 'Dwarf Tossing.' Did you return to California to live on a commune and grow weed?"

"No, there was nothing here to come back to so I stayed in Chicago for a few more years. I realized that the only way to get out of my shit-hole-of-a-life was to go to school and get some kind of a degree. I started taking IT classes at a small tech school on the south side of Chicago."

"Where did you get the money to pay for your education, Jimmy?"

"Because I'm a dwarf, my disability opened a lot of doors for me. I found grants and scholarships through a group called the Little People of America. I never paid a penny out of my own pocket. I owe a lot to the LPA."

"Did Angus go to school too?"

"No, he was dumb as a box-a-rocks. He ended up back on his family's farm, bustin' mules."

"Jimmy, for Christ's sake, what the hell are you talking about? Busting mules?"

"Back in the day, Angus' family was big in the mule business. Mules were used to harvest oysters at the various grow out facilities along Tomales Bay, and his family provided them." Jimmy cleared his throat and then he went on. "Before the mules could be sold, they had to be domesticated, enough at least to take a lead and trust their handlers. Otherwise they'd kick 'em right square in the nads – and that's an awful sight."

"So that's called 'mule bustin'?"

"Well first the mule has to learn they can trust the guy behind 'em, the one with the reins. Since I was a lot lighter than Angus, they would mount me bareback on the mule. I'd kick the heels of my rubber boots into their ribs and hang on for the ride. Angus would try to steady the animal with a rope tied around its neck. By and by, the mule would get used to me. Once he did, I'd hop off on a tree stump or the fence rail surrounding the corral."

"How many mules did you end up bustin' with your cousin, Angus?"

"In the heyday of the oyster business, the grow-outs would buy four or five mules a month."

"Jimmy, I'm confused. Does this have anything to do with your mother?"

"Sure. When I was a kid, my mother brought men into the house and 'entertained' 'em all night long – if you know what I mean. I'd listen to 'em goin' at it from the next room. I was too small to stop em' – as if she wanted to stop anyway – the anger built inside and I took it out on the mules."

"I'm not following."

"My mother screwed me up but I couldn't get even with her. Sometimes, my anger turned to rage when I worked with the mules."

"That's awful, Jimmy. Did you use a whip on the mules? What role did Angus play?"

"No. Angus would grab the reins and force 'em to stand still – ya' know, he was stronger than any mule. I'd grab a baseball bat and beat the livin' shit out of that poor animal. That's why we call it 'mule bustin'. Once he was beaten a few times, that mule was ready to work the oyster beds."

"Did you and Angus get paid much for bustin' those mules?"

"Some. His parents gave us a few bucks now and then, but not a lot. We was all poor back then."

"When was the last time you talked to Angus?"

"I'm not sure. I guess it's been at least five years since I've seen him...it was back in Tomales."

Johnson changed the subject abruptly and asked, "How'd you lose your job at Cal-DOT, Jimmy?"

"The Cal-DOT bitches denied my free speech rights. They were way too 'PC' for their own good."

"What kind of stuff were you saying?"

"You know, stuff. Like complaining about all the hours I had to work."

"That's it?"

"Well I made sure to let 'em know that the girls in the office were held to different standards. They could come and go whenever they wanted and when it was time to do an install or major system test, I was the one that gave up my nights and weekends to be there. Never the girls."

"So, in your opinion, the women were treated better than you were?"

"Yes, they really were, along with all of those dot-heads."

"Who?"

"Those Indian contractors the state hires to save money – save money my ass. They do a shit job writing code and install it without testing it. They'd just dump it in and I had to clean up their mess."

"Too bad they won't have you to kick around anymore, Jimmy."

"Damn right. They just don't know it yet."

"Jimmy, what can you tell me about your lady friend, Lorraine Cordiva? Like how did you two meet and when?"

"Look, Detective. I'm late for a meeting. Am I under arrest or not?"

"Jimmy, I just have a couple more questions for you. If you cooperate and answer them, you'll be free to go. Otherwise we can do this at the station."

"Fine. Okay. I met Lorraine a few years ago on the campus of the Dominican University in San Rafael. She was a little shy about dating a dwarf, that is until she tangled with Jumbo Johnson..."

"Jimmy. Who the hell is Jumbo Johnson?"

"Well, genius, if I let Jumbo out of his cage, I'd be arrested for assault with a really big weapon."

Johnson walked away scratching his head. *Who or what is Jumbo Johnson? If it's a real guy, how does he fit into the case?*

* * *

Johnson went to the address Paula had given him for Lorraine Cordiva's apartment in San Rafael. Before entering, he decided to do a web search to validate Jimmy's story about dwarf tossing. He found an old article by Mike Royko, of the Chicago Tribune, that corroborated Jimmy's "Chicago Dwarf Tossing" story. Then he did a search on "Jumbo Johnson." The first article that came up was about President Lyndon Johnson. The president often referred to his male member as "Jumbo." *That little shit might be telling the truth?* Johnson was beginning to soften on Jimmy and was thinking that his alibi was on the level. He might not have been involved with the Tomales fires at all. *Who might be responsible for them if Jimmy's clean?*

Finally he did a search on "Lorraine Cordiva" to try and validate Jimmy's story about her being a student at Dominican. He did not find a match. *Actually, Jimmy never said she was a student at Dominican. All he said was that they met on the campus.*

He was anxious to talk to Lorraine Cordiva to see if she could confirm Jimmy's alibi. If he did have a rock-solid alibi, Johnson would suggest that Jimmy be removed from the list of suspects.

Johnson was shot about eight weeks ago and today was his first time back in the field since that shooting. He had a difficult time catching his breath after chasing down Jimmy. His heart was pounding and he was sweating profusely. *What in the hell is happening? Am I really that out of shape?*

He called Chao to say "Hi" and give her a quick update on his day. He also had something to tell her but for the life of him, he could not remember what it was...

Chapter 16

"Hey, Babe. It's me..."

"Mark, I'm so glad you called. I miss you..."

"I miss you too, Chao. How's your day goin'?"

"It's fine. I was just about to call you to see what time you'll be home?"

"Why? What's up?"

"Nothing much, I just miss you, Mark."

"Let's see...I've got a meeting with Paula at three to compare notes on the arson case. I'm guessing I'd be home no later than five thirty or so. OK?"

"That's fine, Mark. It's just that Melli called to say that she and Marvin want us to come for dinner tonight at seven. I told her I had to call you to see if you would be available." Marvin, Chao's brother, is a FOREX trader. After graduating with an advanced degree in finance from Berkeley, he began trading foreign currencies. Marvin was very successful. His office was in the financial district with a beautiful view of the Bay Bridge. Chao knew that Johnson was intimidated by Marvin's success. He has money and flaunts it...the complete opposite of Johnson. They live in a beautiful home in the St. Francis Wood neighborhood – the other side of the tracks from Johnson's home in the Sunset District.

"Chao, that's fine. He's your brother and it's been a while since we've seen them. It was probably back before I was shot."

"A lot has changed since then..." Chao said with a sigh, recalling the day he was shot. Changing the subject, she asked, "How's your first day back?"

"Okay, I guess." Johnson didn't want to alarm Chao, and hesitated telling her about his accelerated heartbeat. "I do miss relaxing in the garden with you, Chao. I miss spending my days with you."

"That's sweet, Mark. Now tell me why you really called. What's on your mind?" Chao had a sixth sense. She could always tell when Johnson was keeping something from her.

"I'm really out of shape. I had to chase down a suspect today, a dwarf. My heart was racing and I'm still trying to catch my breath. It damn near killed me, Chao."

"Mark, you need to see your doctor and get into some sort of a workout routine. Jeez, you do realize his legs are half as long as yours are, right? Were you able to catch him?"

"You mean the dwarf? Of course I caught him. I pinned the little squirt down on the hood of a car while I questioned him."

"I wish I could have seen my big strong Fabio catch that little man..." Chao tried to cover up her giggle but Johnson heard it. It brought a smile to his face from ear to ear. He hadn't heard her giggle in a long time and he missed it. Then she asked, "Mark, how's Paula doing?"

"Paula's taken right over. There's no doubt that she's in charge now."

"I'm glad to hear it, she'll do well." Chao was hoping Paula would take over the homicide desk so Mark could retire without feeling guilty.

"Get this, Chao. Paula's gonna let me keep the artwork from my office."

"Wait. Are you talking about that half naked, fat-assed dancer hanging behind your desk?"

"It's a classic, Chao. She's been with me longer than you have. I'm bringing her home with me."

"Mark, if you bring that thing here, I promise you I'll donate it to some charity – that is, if I can find one with low enough standards to take it."

"Harsh, Chao, very harsh. Look, I gotta run. I'll see you around five thirty. Love you, Babe."

* * *

Johnson walked from his car to the entrance of Cordiva's building. Her apartment was on third and the elevator wasn't working. By the time he reached the halfway point, Johnson began to feel weak and dizzy. When he finally reached the third floor he had to sit on the step for a few minutes to catch his breath. *Chao's right, I really need to get back in shape.*

Johnson was met with the acrid smell of curry hanging in the air as he walked the hall to Cordiva's apartment. *These places really have piss-poor ventilation.* He heard the TV playing inside her apartment and knocked on the door. A woman in her mid-thirties opened the door. "Hello. I'm Detective Mark Johnson with Marin County. I'm looking for a miss Lorraine Cordiva."

"You're in luck, Sugar. You found her."

"I'd like to talk to you about Jimmy..."

Before he could finish his sentence, the woman jumped in, "Jimmy Loomis?"

"Yes. Jimmy Loomis. May I come in?"

"Please do, Inspector."

"And it's 'Detective' not 'Inspector'."

"Oh, sorry. Please come in, Detective." Johnson couldn't help but notice the wide array of sex toys scattered around her apartment – the kind that the working gals in the Tenderloin District would use to pleasure their customers.

"Tell me, Miss Cordiva, what line of work are you in?"

"Look around, Detective and try detecting a little. Now, what do you think I do for a living?"

"Right. I figured you worked in guest relations. Is it okay if I call you Lorraine?"

"Sure you can, Detective. It's a lot better than what most people call me. You said you wanted to talk about Jimmy. What do you want to know?"

"I got the impression from a conversation I had with Jimmy, that you and he are in some sort of "love" relationship. Is that true?"

"Yes we are, every Tuesday at three-thirty sharp. I love him until he screams for me to stop."

"Wait a minute. You screw him for money? But he has you named as the beneficiary on his life insurance policy."

"Detective, I screw lots of guys 'for money' as you put it. I'll screw you too if you got cash. Hell, I may even give you a free sample if you want."

Lorraine was wearing a black silk top with thin spaghetti straps. She was a well-proportioned girl of Asian-Anglo decent. Her hair was dark and long and it danced atop her shoulders when she moved.

"Ahh – no thanks, Ma'am." Johnson couldn't help being distracted by her wardrobe. "Can we stay focused on Jimmy, please?"

147

"Time is money in my business, Detective. Ask me what you want so I can get back to work."

"How is it you are the beneficiary?"

"No other girl will give the little guy the time of day, but I enjoy his company. Plus, he's absolutely amazing in the sack; one of the best I've ever had. I do look forward to three-thirty Tuesday afternoons, Detective."

Lorraine offered Johnson a chair, a hard, stiff, wooden kitchen chair with a bentwood back. As he sat there, she came to him. Without a word, she straddled her legs to each side of his lap. Then she slowly bent down, got close to his face, and gazed directly into his eyes. He jumped up off the chair. "Knock it off lady. I told you, I'm not interested."

"Sure you are, Detective." She was right. He had become intoxicated by her perfume. It's been a long time since he felt like this. He didn't want it to stop, but he couldn't let it go further. Then she put her lips close to his ear, close enough so he felt her breath on him, warm and gentle. "Mark," she said in a low sultry whisper, "I'm ready for you big guy...and I want you."

He was trapped and ready to reach for her when she whispered in his ear, "I won't tell your wife about the two of us if you name me as the sole beneficiary on your life insurance policy."

"You bitch," Johnson said, pushing her away.

"Perhaps. Detective, I may be a bitch but a girl's gotta' take care of her financial future. I'm named as the beneficiary on life insurance policies for twenty or thirty guys."

"That's fraud, Lorraine."

"Bullshit, Detective. It's my retirement plan."

"You're coercing your johns into paying for the policy in exchange for keeping quiet about their exploits. Well pardon me, lady. You're right. It's not fraud, it's extortion...and guess what? The last time I checked, that's illegal too."

"Everyone dies, Detective. All I'm asking them to do is sign a policy that pays me when they do."

"Tell me why this is not extortion?"

"Because I'm in control of the entire process. I initiate and hold each of the policies and I'm the one who pays the premiums, not the johns. They don't even know the name of the insurance companies I'm using. All they do is sign the initial paperwork and I take it from there."

"How much is each policy worth?"

"Two hundred and fifty grand, Detective."

Johnson thought about it for a minute. *Maybe Lorraine was right. With twenty guys, each one with a policy paying out two hundred fifty grand, she gets about five million bucks over time. That will pay for a lot of batteries...*

"How much do these policies cost you?"

"It comes to about fifteen hundred a month. To keep premium costs low, I make sure the customers I select are in good health and don't smoke. Oh, they have to be younger than forty-five years old too. Sorry Detective, but I guess you're too old to get me a good rate."

Being the professional that he is, Johnson let the age comment slide. Still sweating from the whole ordeal, he knew he had to continue the interview in order to validate Jimmy's alibi. "Jimmy claims you traveled to Chicago with him. He said that the two of you were there on December first of this year. Is that correct Miss Cordiva?"

"No way in hell, Detective. First of all, I hate the cold. But more importantly, I have a strict policy to never go anywhere with any of my clients – it can get really strange. It's way too dangerous. That little shit played you like a fiddle."

Chapter 17

"Paula? Hey. It's Johnson."

"And hello to you too," Paula said, somewhat miffed by Johnson's lack of social graces.

"When do you think you'll get to the office? I'm almost there now. I've got some new information on Jimmy that I want to go over with you."

"I'll be there in twenty minutes or so...around two-thirty." *Why did I take this job? It seems like I'm always in the car.* Paula was driving back from the Tomales area when she took Johnson's call.

"Perfect, let's meet to discuss the case when you get here. Is that okay? I'll invite Jurek to join us too, if you're ok with that."

"Sure, Mark. Fine. But I'm starving. I was going to stop for a burger first. It'll be closer to three before I get there."

"I'm close to a Tony's 'Down and Out Burger.' I'd be happy to stop and pick something up for you; a burger and whatever else you might want."

"Sounds good, Mark. I'll take a double cheese, ah...make it Swiss. With grilled onions, a side of fries and a diet whatever."

"I've also got news to share with you about Jimmy's lady friend, Lorraine Cordiva."

"Okay, can't wait. See you in the office."

Johnson was only ten minutes from the Sheriff's Office when he pulled into the drive-through lane at Tony's. It was one of those "throw back" places, one of the first drive-through restaurants in Marin County. The burgers were greasy but hit the spot.

The first step in placing an order was to drive up to the speaker. It was set in the face of an old clown wearing a plaid shirt and a fedora. The microphone was his nose, the speaker his mouth. *Johnson smiled, is this the real Tony?* Johnson placed his order and wondered how anyone could ever understand the garbled voice coming over the speaker. He paid the girl at the window. She handed him his order and to his amazement, they had it right.

Johnson arrived at the office before Paula and found Jurek in the squad room. The two of them began to list their observations on the whiteboard.

1: Jimmy hates his mother
2: Jimmy will inherit his mother's estate
3: Jimmy lied about his alibi
4: Jimmy's girlfriend is a prostitute

Paula arrived a few minutes later. "Hi, Guys. Let's eat. I'm starving." She studied the board while eating her burger and sipping the diet cola. Then she said, "Mark, where's the damn ketchup? I gotta' have ketchup with my fries."

Johnson rummaged through the drawers of the squad-room desk. "Here," he said, tossing a couple of wrinkled looking ketchup packets to her, "It's the best I can do."

"Gee, thanks. I see you started the profile on Jimmy. Got any hunches yet? Do you think he did it? Is he capable of starting those fires?"

"Yes to all three, Paula. But before we can name him as a suspect we need some hard evidence tying him, or anyone else for that matter, to the fires. Sure, he's got a motive and he's also a liar but that doesn't make him an arsonist...or a killer."

"Right. Let's call Jonah to see if his team found any prints or DNA evidence that matches Jimmy's." Paula called Jonah and asked if he could join them. Then she turned to Jurek, "Can you run a bar-code trace from the kerosene canisters that were found at the fire? Maybe we can catch a break that way."

"I'll go down to the lab and get it started," said Jurek. "But, remember, sometimes a barcode trace is like looking for a needle in haystack. I'll keep you posted on what we find."

"Ya' know," Johnson said, "Jimmy seemed to be on the level at first. He told me how he and his cousin, Angus got involved in Dwarf Tossing back in Chicago some thirty years ago."

"If you fell for that load of crap, Mark, I've got a sheep farm I'd like to sell you."

"Paula," Johnson said reaching for his phone, "I'm forwarding you an old article that appeared in the Chicago Tribune. It's about Dwarf Tossing. A reporter named Mike Royko wrote it years ago. It's exactly how Jimmy described it. It all checked out."

"Come on, Mark. Really? Do you think it might be possible that Jimmy read the same article and then built his bullshit alibi around it?"

"I don't know, I guess. I also stopped to see his girlfriend – Lorraine Cordiva."

"The people at Cal-DOT made it sound like those two were inseparable. She's even a named beneficiary on his life insurance policy."

"Paula, the gal's a hooker with an interesting angle. She coerces her johns into naming her the sole beneficiary on their life insurance policies. She'll collect over five million after they all die."

"That sounds illegal, Mark."

"That's what I thought too. I told her it sounded like extortion to me."

"Exactly."

"Then she told me that *she's* the one who pays the premiums. She'll collect on the policy when the john dies. She calls it her retirement plan."

"I da' know, Mark. It still sounds fishy to me."

"I agree, Paula. So, did you learn anything about Jimmy's cousin, Angus McGee?"

"We can't get to him without paperwork. His parents are very protective and refuse to let him talk to strangers – especially strangers with badges. They wouldn't let me in the house. I had to wait on the stoop. They're hiding something."

"Did you ask them about the four canisters of kerosene Angus bought at the general store?"

"I did. His mother told me that they use it to heat their barn. I asked if I could do a quick walk through the barn. I wanted to see if they really use a kerosene heater."

"Did you find one?"

"Didn't get in. I was told to come back with a search warrant. I've started the process to obtain one. I hope to get it soon."

"Good, let me know when you have it. I'd like to go with you. Jimmy was telling me how he and Angus worked on the family's mule farm. Did you notice any mules at their farm?"

Before Paula could respond, Dr. Chiang walked in. "Jonah," said Chen, "We're wondering if you have any crime scene evidence that would connect either of our suspects to the fires."

"Paula," said Chiang, "I'm pleased to see that you don't see a need to waste time on formalities for old friends. Just jump right in why don't ya'..."

"I'm sorry. You're right." Paula walked over to Chiang and gave him a hug. Johnson, Chiang and Chen had known each other for many years. The three had attended Lowell High School together.

"It's great to have you on board, Paula."

"Thanks, Jonah. I'm looking forward to working with you. We have a person of interest and he has a motive. We're hoping there's evidence that might link him to the Tomales fires."

"Physical evidence, DNA or prints, from any of the fires that might be useful?" Asked Johnson.

"Well, guys. There wasn't much. I walked the Loomis fire scene with Grotowski shortly after the fire had been knocked down. Have you worked with him before?"

"No. He's partnering with us on the Tomales case. I am impressed with him so far," said Chen.

"He did a good job describing *how* each of the fires had been staged," added Johnson. "There's no doubt it was arson. Now we need something solid, some sort of hard evidence, that will tie the arsonist to the scene and maybe tell us *who* did it."

"Or eliminate 'who didn't' do it," added Chen.

"Like I said, Mark. There wasn't a lot there. But we did find a couple of things at the scene," said Chiang. "For starters, we found kerosene cans that were left by the arsonist. I saw Jurek heading to the lab to run bar-code checks on them."

"Hopefully the bar-codes can tell us where those cans were purchased," said Johnson.

"We did find latent prints on the shovel used to jam the door shut at the fire that claimed Grace Loomis," added Chiang.

"You found prints on the shovel?" asked Chen.

"Yes, and they matched those that were found on one of the kerosene cans at the Donegras fire."

"So the same fingers were at both fires. That's big," said Chen.

"Do the prints match either of the two victims?"

"No they don't, Mark" said Jonah. "They belong to a third party, someone who may have set the fires. Perhaps the arsonist?"

"Paula's been to the McGee farm to learn what she could about Angus and his association with his cousin, Jimmy Loomis," added Johnson.

"Like I told Mark, Angus McGee's mother was extremely protective. She wouldn't allow me talk to Angus at all. However, she did say that Angus and Loomis were close friends when they were teens."

Johnson added, "She didn't notice mules on the farm either."

"What in the hell are you talking about, Mark?"

"Jonah," said Johnson. "The McGee's raised mules. It was actually a pretty big operation in its day. Jimmy and Angus would domesticate the mules so the family could sell them to the local oyster companies. They were used to haul in racks of oysters to be harvested from the grow-out beds."

Chen asked, "I assume the canisters found at the scene tested positive for kerosene? If Jurek is able to trace the UPC codes to the point of purchase, we could review video surveillance of the cash registers to help us identify the buyer or buyers."

"Yes, they tested positive," replied Jonah.

"The clerk at the Tomales General Store told me that Angus had been in recently and purchased four canisters of kerosene," said Paula.

"If the bar codes are traced to the general store, we've got a strong evidence. We still need to know if the prints on those kerosene cans belong to Angus or Jimmy. If they do, case closed," said Jonah.

"Oh, I almost forgot. Angus' mother told me that Angus and Jimmy Loomis met for lunch a few months ago," said Chen.

"Wait a minute." Johnson was livid. "Jimmy told me he hasn't seen Angus for a few years."

"Sounds like you guys have enough to take the next step. Just sayin'..." said Jonah.

"Jonah's right, Mark. We need to bring Jimmy and Angus in and take a look at their fingerprints."

"I've already issued the warrants," said Johnson.

"By the way," added Chiang. "I ran a search of the victims on the state's medical record database."

"What's that used for?" asked Chen.

"The state uses it to track various things from immunizations to infectious diseases to cancer, etc. The Greater Bay Area Cancer Registry (GBACR) is a subset of the larger State of California database. It's standard procedure to check the database when we do an autopsy."

"So what did you learn?" asked Chen.

"Our two victims were listed as people currently being treated for cancer in the nine-county area, and that includes Marin County."

"What about HIPPA?" Johnson asked.

"What about it? The information is stored in a way that protects privacy. Since I'm the Medical Examiner, I can access the details. It turns out that both victims, Donegras and Loomis, had recently been diagnosed with a rare form of Leukemia. They were terminal with just a few months to live."

"Interesting, Jonah. Since both of them were close to death, why would anyone want to risk killing them intentionally? It doesn't make sense."

"Good point, Paula," said Johnson. "Jonah, you said that this is a rare form of Leukemia. What makes it rare?"

"It's known as chronic myeloid leukemia," said Jonah. "Often, but not always, this form of leukemia can be linked to some sort of radiation exposure, typically plutonium, the type used to manufacture nuclear weapons."

"What the hell?" said Chen, "How, or better yet, where did these two women get exposed to that?"

"The research is not conclusive," said Chiang. "This cancer may be caused by other factors too."

"Sure, Jonah. I get it. However, the coincidences are starting to shape a story for me. They had worked together for years and lived in the same tiny town – in the same houses, in fact – for years."

"I agree, Mark. This looks like it's more than a coincidence. It requires a deeper look. We've got a few more facts for the whiteboard." Chen got up, walked over to the whiteboard, reached for the black marker and wrote down the following:

5: The victims worked together for years
6: They lived in close proximity to each other
7: Both were diagnosed with the same cancer
8: Both were terminal with a short time to live
"Do you have anything to add, Mark?"

Johnson then took a turn at the board, "We're generating some new facts that are leading to more questions." Under the heading of the "Knowledge Gap" Johnson added the following questions:

1: Is their cancer a motive for murder?

"That's a good question, Mark. We didn't even know about their illness initially," said Paula.

"Right – let me go on. I'm on a roll." Johnson added the next few questions without interruptions.

2: Was Jimmy/Angus involved in their deaths?
3: Is the arsonist working for a third party?
4: Was La Ostra, LLC involved in this?
5: Is the radiation from the Farallones?

"Is it okay to comment Mark?"

"Sure, Paula. I'm done for the moment."

"You're right. We've got a lot more questions than answers," said Chen. "Is it possible that the radiation at the Farallones caused these cancers? If so, how probable is it? Even if the radioactive waste dumped at the Farallones caused the cancer, there's zero probability that those islands waltzed into Tomales and started the fires that killed them."

It is common knowledge that, shortly after the end of World War II, the U.S. Military dumped fifty thousand barrels of radioactive waste in the waters surrounding the Farallon Islands. These islands are thirty miles west of San Francisco and just twenty miles from the point where the sea enters Drakes Bay, the home of the Dream Bay Oyster Company.

"Two victims, same cancer, no coincidence," said Paula. "We must stay focused on the strongest leads that we have for now. We could really drift off base if we're not pragmatic."

"Right, Paula. Let's drill down on Jimmy and Angus as soon as they arrive."

"Jonah, can you dig into the radiation question to help us understand the chances that these cancers resulted from the waters around the Farallones?"

"Sure thing, Paula. I'll see what I can find out."

Chapter 18

"Guys. I've got some bad news," said Jonah as he returned to the squad room. "The prints found at the scene don't match Jimmy or Angus."

"What? Where do we go now?" asked Paula, frustrated by the news. She needed something that would link Jimmy and Angus to the fires. Also, the discovery that each victim was suffering from end-stage cancer caused her to re-evaluate the motive. "Their cancers have to be a material piece of any motive we develop." Then in a tone of surrender she said, "This case is not making any sense, Mark. The women were going to die anyway, why would someone risk prison time by killing them?"

"I don't know, Paula. But I think we've become trapped by our assumptions instead of the facts. We need to go back a few steps, look at the facts first and then let the data lead the way. We got ahead of ourselves focusing on Jimmy without the evidence to back it up. It was too easy."

"Your right. Fact one, we have two women who died as a direct result of arson. Right?"

"Yes, and we also know they worked together at the oyster factory for years."

"Their homes were recently purchased by the La Ostra, LLC."

"I still think Jimmy and Angus are involved in some way. Jimmy's constant lies, coupled with Angus' family covering for him, tell me they're guilty of something. But, we can't hold 'em much longer without charging 'em."

"I agree. We need to dig deeper and do it fast. These guys are hiding something. I can taste it."

Johnson began searching for Jimmy's name on the multi-jurisdictional Law Enforcement databases he has access to. Finally he got a hit. He found him on the National Crime Information Center (NCIC) database, created by the FBI. NCIC is used by law enforcement and criminal justice agencies tasked with finding stolen property, fugitives, and missing persons. Johnson called out to Paula, "Wow. Take a look at this."

"What'd ya' find, Mark."

"It seems that Jimmy was involved in a shooting a few years ago on the UCSF campus. There were a total of five students killed by some goofy-assed, deranged gunman."

"I remember that incident," said Paula. "All of the victims were women, some were Indian. Does it say who the shooter was or what became of him?"

"The shooter took his own life while holding a hostage. Guess who the hostage was?"

"Jimmy?"

"Ding-ding-ding. You win the prize, Paula."

"No shit? Our Jimmy?"

"Yup."

"Wait a minute, Mark. Does it make sense to you that someone would go through the trouble of grabbing a hostage and then take their own life?"

"No, it doesn't. The rationale for taking a hostage is to create an escape shield. Paula, chew on this for a minute: maybe Jimmy acted out his hatred of women and minorities and killed those people at UCSF himself. What if he was the shooter?"

"You just told me that the shooter took his own life. Didn't you?"

"That's what the report said, Paula. However, there are other facts, validated by witnesses, which the investigation ignored. First, Jimmy *was* at the scene. Second, shots were fired. Third, there was a hostage situation. Finally, six people ended up dead, including the shooter."

"Mark, it sounds like you are forming one of your hunches. Spit it out please, keep going..."

"Stay with me on this. What if Jimmy was the shooter? He takes a hostage and then shoots him. He makes it appear that the hostage was actually the shooter. Next, he places the gun in the hostage's hand and fires it one last time and then declares to the world that the shooter took his own life."

"That's brilliant, Mark. The victim's prints end up on the murder weapon and gunpowder residue is on his hand. Jimmy walks away and the rest of the world thinks the shooter took his own life."

"That little shit's a genius, Paula."

"Did you find any eyewitness statements in the case report to support your theory? How did the witnesses describe what *they* saw and heard?"

"There are a few that don't jive with the final ruling. For example, *none* of the witnesses actually saw the shooter's face. One witness noted that she 'saw someone shooting from behind a parked car but couldn't see his face.' This is interesting."

"Interesting because...?"

"Well, when I found Jimmy earlier today, I saw him running between some parked cars in the lot adjacent to his apartment building. I couldn't see his face either; at least not clearly enough to recognize him, he's too short. What if it was a dwarf shooting from behind the parked car? What if it was *Jimmy* who the witnesses had actually seen?"

"Interesting, Mark. What else...?"

"Another witness mentioned there was a lull of a few seconds between the final two shots."

"That also supports your theory, Mark, in two ways. First of all, suicide victims rarely, if ever, shoot themselves twice."

"Duh. Once usually does it."

"Second, it supports the idea that Jimmy did shoot the hostage. After shooting him, it took a few seconds for Jimmy to put the gun in the dead guy's hand and squeeze off one final round into the air."

"That explains why only one slug was found at the scene, not two."

"Does the report indicate which agency led the investigation?"

"The FBI was leading it, Paula."

"I remember the incident, Mark. It took place about eight years ago outside Health Sciences on the UCSF campus at Sixteenth and Third."

"We could continue digging but it's not our problem. It's a cold case now. We should notify the San Francisco PD and FBI to share your theory."

"I agree. We need to stay focused on the arson investigation. I'll put a call into the SFPD suggesting they reopen the files on the campus shooting case."

"Good idea. Plus, it will give us a reason to keep Jimmy locked up for a while longer," said Johnson.

"Right. I think that little shit is behind the fires, Mark. I'm just not sure why, what his role was or how to prove it. It's just a gut feeling I have."

"What about Angus?"

"We don't have enough to hold him. We have to cut 'em lose – we can always pick him up again if we need to talk to him."

Johnson glanced at the clock. It was four forty-five. With a worried look on his face he explained, "I need to red-light it home. Chao is expecting me at five-thirty."

"No problem. We had a pretty good day. Plus we stumbled onto a new perspective for the campus shooting. I never felt the initial findings held water."

"But we're not any closer to solving our arson case, Paula. That has to be our priority."

"Agreed. We need to dig deeper into how the two victims were connected."

"I'll call lock-up and ask them to cut Angus loose but hold Jimmy a little longer."

"Thanks, Mark. Statutes require the prosecutor charges Jimmy within forty-eight hours of his arrest or he walks. I'll contact the DA and fill him in."

"What was the name of the LLC that owns the properties?" Johnson's mind was drawing a blank, "Was it La Strata or something like that? I think it might tie into this case in some way too."

"It's La Ostra, LLC. I'd like the two of us to drive up to Eureka in the morning to check out their story. I want to know why they bought those three properties from Loomis and Donegras. I'll drive if you don't mind."

"Sounds good. Pick me up at nine?"

"I'll be there at eight-thirty. We'll stop for coffee along the way. Now, you get home to Chao, I don't want her on my case. I'll touch base with Jurek and see if he's made any progress with the barcodes."

* * *

"Hi, Jurek. Wow, this is the first time in the lab for me...very impressive. I wanted to check to see if you made progress on the barcodes yet?"

"I've spent the past two hours in the lab going over the data. The trace indicated that the UPC codes on those cans were last scanned at a C-Mart store in Rohnert Park."

"Where's Rohnert Park?"

"It's just north of Petaluma, about twenty-five miles from Tomales. I'm heading to the store to get a copy of their register tapes. Maybe we'll get lucky."

"Good work, Jurek. Let me know what you come up with."

Chapter 19

Johnson sat outside his house waiting for Paula. *Where the hell is she? She was supposed to be here by now. I hope being late isn't part of 'the new Paula.'* Usually prompt, she was nearly fifteen minutes late. Finally, she pulled up in front of the house.

"Hi, Paula. Sleep in?" Johnson hates it when people are late. It put him in a snarly mood.

"Sorry I'm late but I had to stop for gas," she said as Johnson approached car. "I also picked us up some coffee for us so we don't have to waste time stopping along the way."

"Do you have any idea where we're going? Eureka's a pretty large town."

"No, Mark. Maybe we, well you that is, could find the address for La Ostra, LLC on your phone while we're driving. We'll also need an address and directions to the Eureka Police Department as well as the Humboldt County Sheriff's Office. I think we should start with the Sheriffs Office."

"Anything else I can do for you?" Johnson was struggling with Paula being in charge and his tone reflected it. "Have you ever been to Eureka?"

"First timer. How about you?"

"Chao and I took the kids up that way a few times. It's kind of a dull drive until we get to Willits. The scenery changes at that point from the drab rolling prairie, to mountains and giant redwoods."

"How far is Willits?"

"I think it's about half way. Probably two and a half hours from here. Maybe we could stop there for a bio-break and grab some lunch."

"That would be about eleven thirty; a little too early for lunch."

"If you want to drive another hour past Willits, there's a nice cafe in Garberville."

"Sounds good. Let's plan to stop there for gas too." The two were silent for the next half hour.

Johnson broke the silence, "Have you ever seen that giant redwood? The one cars drive through."

"Yeah, in pictures. What about it?"

"Well, that's along the way. Pretty cool. I'll try to get the location and directions."

"Mark, we are on official police business; not a vacation. We need to act professional."

"Got it, Paula. Maybe we should put together a list of the objectives we want to achieve in Eureka."

"Ok. Take your notebook out and start writing. For starters, we need to learn as much as we can about La Ostra. Start with operations: Do they own other properties? If so, where are they? What's the business model driving cash flow and is it legal?"

"I'll search their Articles of Organization. I have access to it on the state database. I also want to know about the background of the founders? Do they show up on the criminal records database? All this stuff should be searchable."

"Hopefully you can do a search for answers before we get up there."

"Great thought, Paula. Except for the fact that we've got zero bars here right now...no service."

"Crap."

* * *

They had been driving for about two hours and forty-five minutes when they arrived in Willits. It was there that Highway 101 detoured through town due to road construction. A large banner with the words, "Willits: Gateway to the Redwoods" hung on a cable spanning Main Street suspended between two buildings on either side of the street.

"Mark. Do you need to stop or can you go for another hour or so?"

171

"I'm good. Keep going. I'm getting a few bars now. I'll see what I can find out about the LLC."

Paula kept driving. Willits has a "cowboy" look and feel to it, which makes sense since agriculture is big in these parts. Exiting town, she found her way back onto the 101. The scenery, as Johnson had predicted, changed to redwoods and mountains. A low-lying fog had formed. Drifting in and out of the eighty-foot treetops, creating a beautiful scene.

"How'd you do on the web search, Mark? Find anything that might be useful?"

"I did get some names but lost my connection before I could run a background check on them."

"What names did you find?"

"I got two names, Jackobus McDermott, a.k.a. "Jacko" McDermott and Paddy Burke. Do they ring any bells with you, Paula?"

"I wonder if that Burke character is an alias for Leo Burke? He's the last remaining fugitive from a bombing that ended up killing a researcher back east, in Wisconsin I think, forty-some years ago."

"I'll double check when I get back on line but I think the bomber's name is Burt, Leo Burt, with a 'T'. I was in grade school when that bombing took place. However, a few years ago there was an alert in the Bay Area. One of the bombers had been spotted in the Oakland area. It may have been Burt."

"It could be the same guy but probably not. If it were, why in the hell would he put his name on the LLC papers? Too easy to get caught; those names get scanned into the FBI's databases."

"You're right, Paula. Fugitives that have evaded capture for as long as he has tend to be pretty smart and don't take risks – either that or they're dead."

* * *

"Whoa. Check it out. That sign says 'Chandelier Tree Next Exit.' That's it, Paula – the drive-through tree. Let's go see it. Come on, what do ya' say?"

"Fine. But you pay the admission fees and don't expect to get reimbursed either."

"OK – deal."

Paula took the Leggett exit. The park with the drive-through tree was a half-mile off the highway. Johnson gave her five bucks for the admission fee. The tree was just a short drive down an old logging road. There were two cars in front of them waiting for their turn to drive through the tree. After a short wait it was their turn.

The "Chandelier Tree" was about three hundred feet tall and over twenty-five hundred years old. The opening in the tree was barely big enough for a sedan to fit through. The minivan in front of them had to back out because it was too tall and too wide for the opening. That meant that Paula and Johnson had to back out too. This delay really aggravated Paula. Finally, she drove ahead, inching her way through the tree. It was a tight fit but she made it without scratching the car. She then turned to Johnson and asked, "Satisfied?"

"Yes. Thanks. Great memories. Can you park by the gift shop? I need to use the facilities."

*　*　*

Thirty minutes after getting back on the 101, they arrived in Garberville. "Let's look for a café or someplace for lunch." The town was full of scraggly looking campers – they were everywhere. "I don't remember it being this crowded when Chao and I were here with the kids."

"That was a long time ago. Things change."

"They sure do. I remember a small café on the main drive." A moment later Johnson pointed too the Woodrose Café. "There it is, over on the right. It's been in business since the fifties." Their parking karma was with them as a nearby parking space opened up. "This place has a healthy menu. There are a ton of 'campers' inside," said Johnson using air quotes on the word camper. "Let's try it."

"Mark, we're in Mendocino County, it has the highest per capita number of pot growers in the U.S. There are literally hundreds of growing operations in the hills with little interference from the cops."

"Uh...I hate to be a stickler, Paula. We're not in Mendocino County any longer. We crossed the line into Humboldt County a little bit ago."

"Whatever. Humboldt's a haven for pot growers too. The 'campers' are here growing weed. Please, order a BLT or a turkey sandwich for me, I'm going to call Jurek to see how his UPC search is going."

"No problem."

Paula took advantage of the cell coverage. "Hi, Jurek. Paula here. Anything yet?"

"Paula, hello. Yeah, I got a large box of register tapes from the C-Mart. I asked for receipts for the week or so before the fire. If I don't find kerosene purchases in this batch of receipts, I'll go back a few days earlier."

"Sounds good, Jurek. Did you find out if they keep video records of the customers at each of the registers?"

"They do. The manager said they keep them for a minimum of two months, longer if they're needed for an investigation. Once I find the exact time and day the kerosene was purchased, we can pinch down the number of the video files we need to go over."

175

"Keep on it, Jurek. Johnson and I are just about to Eureka. We'll be back late tonight. Talk in the morning."

* * *

Johnson found the Sheriff's Office in Eureka on Fourth Street. They entered the building, introduced themselves and asked if they could talk to one of the detectives. They were introduced to Detective Wallace Frasier, a veteran of more than thirty years. After the formalities, Chen and Johnson proceeded to give Frasier an overview of their investigation.

"We're investigating a serial arsonist in Marin County. Three fires with similar MO's were set recently. Two people died. The trail leads here, to Eureka, specifically to the La Ostra, LLC," said Chen.

"So, three fires and two dead? Why do you think La Ostra had anything to do with the fires?" asked Detective Frasier.

"I was told by the land office in Tomales that the La Ostra, LLC has recently purchased all three of the structures," said Chen.

"And the Articles of Organization for the LLC show that their operating address is here in Eureka," added Johnson. "Have you heard of La Ostra?"

"I sure have," replied Frasier. "But most of their holdings in Eureka are related to the oyster business, hence the name, La Ostra...Spanish for oyster."

"What can you tell us about the people behind the business?" asked Chen.

"Well for starters," said Frasier, "The two guys that run that LLC are solid citizens. They've been a key part of the Eureka 'revival' for most of the past ten years."

"Revival?" asked Johnson.

"Yup," said Frasier. "The town was hit hard by the financial crash a few years back. Crabbing was a huge business for us but local crabbers went under due to reduced demand, rising costs, and too many over extended mortgages. The two guys that started La Ostra, McDermott and Burke, had big money, lots of it. They bought up most of the crab boat fleet and processing facilities along Humboldt Bay. They hired the out-of-work crabbers too – well, as many as wanted to work with oysters that is."

"Where can we find these guys?" asked Chen.

"Not exactly sure, Ma'am. A year or so back, Burke and McDermott dropped out of circulation. Some say they're living at a commune on a pot farm near Ferndale. Others say they're swishy and..."

"We don't need to get into that," said Chen, cutting him off. "It's pretty eccentric behavior if you ask me, just walking away from a major investment like that. I thought most of the oyster growing in this state took place down south, on Tomales Bay."

"That used to be the case, Detective Johnson."

"I'm Detective Chen," said Paula. Pointing to Johnson she said, "He's Detective Johnson."

"Sorry for that, Ma'am. What I've been told is that about five years ago, the feds clamped down on the Tomales Bay growers. They'd been given long-term leases over a hundred years ago but recently, the National Park Service had decided to turn the Tomales Bay area into a wilderness reserve. By not renewing the leases, they effectively terminated any and all oyster operations along Tomales Bay."

"So, the oyster business moved from Tomales to Humboldt Bay?" asked Johnson. "Pretty shrewd strategy on the part of La Ostra, don't you think?"

"Yes. The bulk of West Coast oyster growing is based right here in Eureka now. Humboldt Bay has the perfect water, cool and clean, to grow oysters. The crabbing equipment was converted to support oyster growing and also provide an opportunity for the crabbers to feed their families."

"How much of the demand for oysters is now supplied by Humboldt Bay?" Chen asked.

"Like I said, most of California's demand for oysters is supplied from here. A large percentage of the oysters sold in Washington and Oregon come from these parts too. La Ostra, LLC supplied the funding and prospered from that investment."

"Thanks, Detective," said Chen. "Can we visit a couple of the oyster places in Eureka? You know, where the day-to-day work with oysters takes place."

"Sure," replied Frasier. "But you won't see too much. They go out at low tide, harvest a few racks, bring 'em back to the processing facility to rinse and shuck. Or else they grade, bag and ship 'em live."

"That's fine," replied Chen. "I just want to meet some people and get a feel for what it is they do."

"Do you happen to have an address for the last known residence for McDermott and Burke?" asked Johnson. "We would like to speak with them."

"Hang on," said Frasier as he handed Chen a scrap of paper. "Just head on down by the docks to this address. Look for the warehouse with the big 'Blue Points' sign painted on the side of it."

"Thanks," said Chen.

"Now, as far as the address for Burke and McDermott, I'll see what I can find for you. Just stop back here after you visit the processing facility. With luck, I'll have that address and directions for you. However, I'll warn you right now, don't stray off the main roads..."

Chapter 20

Frasier's directions took them south to Ferndale. The scenery was spectacular along that stretch of highway. Giant sequoias and coastal redwoods lined the highway. Red-tailed hawks flew overhead. A low-lying cloud, maybe forty feet up, hung behind the trees framing them in an eerie backdrop.

They took the Ferndale exit onto a two-lane road. "Paula, our next turn is over there," Johnson said, pointing to a poorly marked side road.

"Are you sure?"

"Absolutely, we need to turn onto that road."

"Got it," replied Chen. She made the turn. The gravel road, not heavily traveled, was scattered with fallen branches and other debris from recent storms. "Pretty rough road. I hope we don't get stuck out here. I think we're off the grid, Mark."

"You're right, Paula. No bars out here. We are definitely off the gri..." Before Johnson could finish what he was saying, a shot rang out shattering the rear window on the passenger side. It exploded into tiny glass fragments, hundreds of them, were flying throughout the inside of the car.

"What the...?" Chen said, losing control of the car as it slid into the ditch alongside the road. "Get out," she yelled in a panic. "Somebody's shooting at us and we're sitting ducks out here. Take cover."

"Did you see where that shot came from?" The two were out of the vehicle crouched low behind their doors. Breathless and scared, their weapons were drawn as they looked for the shooter.

"No. The brush is too thick." They couldn't see anyone. The side mirror two inches from Paula's head exploded when the second shot was heard. "Holy shit, Mark. They've got us pinned down out here. Any ideas?"

"Did you happen to see where the second shot came from?" It was apparent from the trajectories that multiple shooters were involved.

"It sounded like it came from ten o'clock off the nose." Then, a third shot. Chen went down. She was lying lifeless next to the car, not moving at all.

"Oh my god. Paula, are you okay?" Paula didn't answer. "Come on Paula, talk to me." Johnson saw blood streaming down her face from an ugly looking wound just above her left ear. *We have to get the hell out of here.*

Johnson, kneeling behind the front passenger door, reached behind him to open the rear door. He crawled up and onto the back seat and over to the driver's side, cutting himself on glass fragments. He slithered out the rear door behind Paula's seat and grabbed her leg. Her limp body was non-responsive, a dead weight, hard to maneuver. He pulled with all his strength, becoming somewhat light-headed in the process. Somehow, he managed to drag her into the back seat, maintaining a low enough profile to stay out of view. He reached back to retrieve her weapon when a fourth shot came. This one took out the back window, showering both of them with another wave of broken glass. Johnson had put his jacket over Paula and then laid on top of her to keep her sheltered. He felt for a pulse. It was weak but he found one.

Then, in what looked like a single motion, he jumped out of the car, shut the rear door and fired a few rounds into the dense underbrush giving him the time he needed to climb into the driver's seat.

Sitting low, Johnson jammed the car into reverse and floored it. Half on and half off the logging road, the car was traveling fast – but in reverse. Johnson couldn't see where he was going. He sensed the driver's side of the car was on paved road and that was all he had to guide him. Traveling fast, close to thirty miles-per-hour, he felt an impact, heard a loud crash and saw the front passenger door fly off. The door had hit a stump on the side of the road and the impact ripped the door off of the hinges. Johnson kept going. A few hundred feet further down the road he found a small clearing and used it to turn the vehicle around. He sped off with three shattered windows, no mirror and a missing front door. He knew he had to get back to Eureka and get Chen to the ER at the local hospital.

"Hey, partner," said Johnson as they pulled into the ER bay. "You're safe now and you'll be fine. Hang in there."

Chen's voice was very weak, "Don't leave me..." She drifted in and out of consciousness as the ER staff carefully removed her from the backseat of the car. "I don't want to die alone..."

* * *

Chen was motionless in the ER for more than three hours, but she was still alive. The monotonous beeping of monitors was reassuring to Johnson. Attentive and concerned, the nursing staff was by her side, trying to get a response from her every five minutes. They would stand at the bedside, squeeze her hand and talk to her face. "Can you hear me,

Ma'am?" asked the nurse. "Ma'am, please. Squeeze my hand if you hear me."

Then, finally, "Of course I can hear you, do you think I'm deaf or something?" asked Paula.

A smile of relief spread across Johnson's face when he heard her. *Paula's gonna be just fine.*

The ER Doc came out to talk to Johnson. "She's lucky to be alive. The bullet grazed the side of her skull but did not penetrate – actually it bounced off. Had it been an inch to the side, we would be taking her to the morgue."

"How long before she can go home?" Johnson asked, relieved that Chen was alive.

"I'm concerned about brain trauma. I want to get a more pictures to understand the severity of any possible cerebral contusion. At the very least we'll keep her over night for observation. If no concerns arise, she could be released tomorrow."

"What about her recovery, Doctor? How long will it take her to recover?"

"Other than a black eye, a bad headache, and sore ribs, she should be fine in a few days."

"That's great news, Doc. Thanks." Standing at Chen's bedside, holding her hand, Johnson smiled and said, "It's a good thing you have a hard head."

"Mark, what the hell happened?" Chen asked, sounding groggy and weak. "We need to get in touch with Frasier and make sure he gets his guys out to those woods."

"I've already done that, Paula. I called him while you were napping. He told me he'd already sent his guys out there. I asked him to call me as soon as he knows something."

"Maybe we should plan on staying over tonight so we can question them tomorrow."

"Ahhh – you're already staying the night, Paula. They want to keep you here for observation. I'll get a room somewhere. I noticed a C-Mart not too far away. Is there anything you need?"

"A clean pair of undies would be nice...white cotton please," she said.

"Right," said Johnson. "Wait, are you serious?"

"Serious? If we're going to work together there's something you need to know...I wear underwear."

When the call came from Frasier, Paula had drifted back to sleep.

"Sure, Detective. Thanks for the call." Johnson was listening intently to what Frasier was saying. "Well, ahh, yes. You bet I'm interested. I'll be there in thirty minutes." Johnson left Paula's car with a dealer for repairs – it would take two weeks. He drove the dealer's loaner to Frasier's office.

"Come in, Detective," said Frasier. "How's she doing? I heard it was pretty bad."

"The doc thinks she'll be fine. Thanks. We're staying in Eureka overnight. Who did this?"

"My guys found a couple of jack-nuts walking in the woods. They were armed with rifles and we believe they are the ones that did the shooting. We questioned them but had to release them."

"What the hell? Who were they working for? McDermott and Burke?" asked an irate Johnson.

"Listen, you didn't follow my directions very well. You took a wrong turn and wandered onto a huge pot farm – those guys were simply protecting their investment."

"How come you won't bust em? Last I heard it was still illegal to grow and sell pot in California."

"Well, Detective, you're in Humboldt County. There are a lot of cannabis cultivators in these hills. If they agree to follow the pending ordinances on pot farming, we agree to leave 'em the hell alone."

"Do the ordinances allow them to shoot at law enforcement? Just an inch to the left and we'd be shipping her body home in a bag." Johnson was furious, pounding his fist on Frasier's desk. "Why in the hell did you release the shooters?"

"Calm down, Detective. Of course we don't like it when law enforcement takes fire. I'm sure you've heard of the 'stand your ground' doctrine. Right?"

"Sure," said Johnson. "But..."

"But nothing. You were on their land without a warrant or probable cause. Plus, you were driving an unmarked car and, according to them, you never announced yourselves as police officers. They were simply protecting what was theirs."

"Fine," said Johnson. "I still want to talk with McDermott and Burke, or are they protected too?"

"No need to be a smartass, Detective. You can go out and see them right now if you want. God knows you can't follow simple directions so how about if I chauffer you out there?"

"Fine. Let's go," said Johnson. He followed Frasier to his squad car and the two headed towards Ferndale to meet Burke and McDermott. Frasier got off the main road about a quarter mile farther than where Johnson had told Chen to turn. "I guess we did get off the road a little before we should have."

"I guess so..." replied Frasier. They were on a winding old logging road that eventually took them into a clearing with log cabins in it. "Welcome to the Ferndale Commune, Detective. It is the last address I had for McDermott and Burke." Frasier drove up to the largest of the cabins. It was huge with two stories and a covered front porch. Johnson and Frasier walked up to the door. Frasier knocked.

"Who the hell is it? Nobody home. Go away," said a cranky voice inside.

"It's Sheriff Frasier. I'm here to talk to Paddy Burke and Jacko McDermott."

"What the hell do you want?" asked the ornery old goat inside.

Frasier recognized the voice. "McDermott," he shouted, "I know it's you. Come out and be social."

The door slowly opened and there he stood. At least six feet four with a full beard, white with age, was Jacobus McDermott. The name Jacobus comes from his English mother, it refers to an old English coin that is no longer used. Jacko, as he was called informally, was wearing nothing but a pair of khaki colored bib overalls. "Okay," said Jacko, "I'm here. Now what the hell do ya' want with me?"

"Mister McDermott, my name is Mark Johnson. I'm a detective from Marin County. We're in the process of investigating a series of arson fires. Three houses were burned down in Tomales and two are dead. All three houses were owned by your LLC."

"I know all about those fires, Detective. They were a total loss for us; we don't have insurance."

"Do you have any idea who would want those structures burned?" asked Johnson.

"Not a clue, Detective. It was Burke's idea to buy them houses in the first place. Maybe you need to go ask him."

"Is Burke around?" asked Frasier.

"Who the hell knows?" responded McDermott.

"Does he live in the commune?" asked Frasier.

"Lately he's either got his nose stuck in his sketch book or he's carving those little birds of his."

"Does he live here?" asked Frasier again.

"Who knows? He's been acting weird lately."

"Mind if I ask some questions?" asked Johnson.

"Damned straight I mind. This place is special and we don't need anyone poking around asking questions." McDermott's response was harsh. He was uncomfortable with the line of questioning.

He's hiding something. "When was the last time you saw Burke?" asked Johnson.

"I 'spose it was a week, maybe ten days ago that I last saw good old Paddy, Detective. We had dinner together."

"How did he seem to you then?" asked Johnson.

"Look, Detective. I don't know. I guess he was fine." McDermott then embellished a bit. "Actually he was acting a little goofy, like he was on 'shrooms or something. Have ya' checked cabin eight yet?"

"Thanks, Jacko," said Frasier, "We'll see if he's in his cabin." A quarter mile up the rocky path was cabin eight. Frasier and Johnson walked up and knocked on the cabin's door. No answer. "Open up, Burke. It's Frasier." He grabbed the door handle and found it unlocked. As he opened the door, the smell from inside the cabin drove him back. He pulled out a handkerchief and held it over his face, "We've got a dead body in here, Johnson. A real stinker." The two men entered to find Paddy Burke lying dead on the floor.

Burke's body was in an advanced stage of decay. His whiskers had grown about three quarters of an inch. His clothes appeared to fit him snuggly, pulled tight from the body's bloat. Maggots, beetles and swarming flies attacked that which remained of his flesh. It was gruesome. A scene that Johnson would not soon forget.

A thin shaft of light was streaming in through the window blinds of the dimly lit cabin. "I'm going outside to call the Medical Examiner," said Frasier.

They opened some windows, searched the cabin for signs of foul play, finding none. Burke's dining table still had a pot of tea on it...long since cold. The contents of the teacup had evaporated and the tea, or whatever was in it, left a dark brown stain inside the cup. The only item out of place was the chair that Burke had been sitting on. It was lying on its side on the floor next to his body. They both assumed that Burke died from a heart attack.

"Can we get an autopsy done?" asked Johnson.

"That'll cost a bundle," said Frasier. "Will Marin County pay for it?"

"Yes, we'll pay for it. Paddy Burke is a person of interest. I need to know how he died."

"Okay, when the ME gets here to remove the remains I'll ask her to do a full autopsy too."

Dr. Jillian James, the County Medical Examiner, arrived twenty minutes later. She was in her mid-thirties with long, amber-colored hair, that she wore down. She had worked with Frasier for years, but reluctantly, she shook his hand acting as if the two didn't know each other. She approached Johnson. He couldn't help but stare at her, captivated by her smile and endless freckles. "Doctor James, I'd like to introduce you to Detective Johnson."

"Please, my friends all call me, JJ," said Doctor James with the slightest little smile.

Johnson reached out his hand saying, "Doctor James, I mean JJ, I'm looking forward to working with you."

"Likewise..."

"Will you be doing a tox test on the residue in the tea cup, Doctor?" Johnson knew that would be an automatic in Marin County.

"Yes, of course," replied Doctor James. "We'll do a full toxicology screening of the liquid and also test tissue samples of the deceased." Johnson was truly impressed by Doctor James. He thought she was very professional too...

"Where are you from?"

"I'm based out of Marin County, JJ"

"I do love the Bay Area, Detective."

On their drive back to Eureka, Johnson asked Frasier about the red flowering bushes along the highway. "What are they called?" he asked, "Those bushes with the red flowers and long leaves."

"They're known as Oleander. The damn things grow like weeds around here. The highway crews planted them years ago as a border shrub along the roads and they really took off. Seems like they grow in all sorts of conditions."

"I've seen them before but really never paid any attention to them," said Johnson. "We've got them down in Marin County too."

"The leaves are long and slender," said Frasier. "It's easy to mistake them for cannabis leaves when they're dried. Just a tad wider."

Chapter 21

I feel like I've been run over. Paula's head began to throb at four in the morning, the pain meds had worn off. Groggy, she wanted out – right now.

Johnson found her sitting on the edge of her hospital bed when he arrived. She still had the IV's inserted in her arms; with lines taped to the back of her hand. An oxygen monitor was clipped to the end of her finger. "Hey stranger," she said when he walked in, "I'm ready to get these tubes out and hit the road. I can't wait to go home."

"It shouldn't be long now, Paula. I saw Doctor Milton in the hallway before I walked in. He said he would be coming in to see you shortly."

"Mark, did they catch the shooters? Did you get a chance to question those bastards?"

"Paula. Ahhh...Frasier's men nabbed two guys and let them go. Stand-your-ground..."

"What the...? They'll be standing *under-ground* if I find 'em."

"Paula, you need to chill. You've been through a lot. I've got new info on McDermott and Burke."

"What did you learn?"

"First off, McDermott is older and quite feeble-minded. At least that was my impression."

"Okay. What about Burke?"

"Well, uh...Burke's dead."

"What? How did that happen?"

"Not sure...found him dead on his cabin floor."

"Any idea what or *who* killed him?"

"We searched the premises and found nothing to indicate foul play. He was drinking a cup of tea one minute and lying dead on the floor the next."

"No indication of a struggle or anything?"

"No. The chair he was sitting on was tipped over but that's it. He'd been dead for a few days when we found him...figured it was his heart. To make sure, I asked the Humboldt County Medical Examiner to do an autopsy."

"So, old man McDermott is all that's left of that La Ostra, LLC? And you think he's a nut-job?"

"I'm afraid so, Paula. He knew about the fires and he knew the properties were a total loss. They were not insured so the LLC had to eat the loss."

"Sounds pretty stupid, if you ask me."

"Or maybe dumb like a fox, Paula."

"What do you mean, Mark?"

"Well, according to Jurek, when an arson loss is insured, anyone who profits from the policy pay-out becomes a potential suspect – it's automatic."

"Right, so then since the LLC didn't insure the properties, they wouldn't be on the suspect list?"

"Exactly, Paula."

"Excuse me...Miss Chen? I'm Doctor Milton. I need to check out your injuries and hopefully we can release you."

"That sounds like a deal, Doctor. Does he need to leave the room?" she asked, pointing to Johnson.

"No, no. Your husband can stay." The doctor looking closely at her head wound said, "It's healing nicely. It looks fine. Change the bandage every day. Now, please remove your gown or lift it up to your neck so I can get a closer look at your ribs. Then we'll get the nurse in to remove the IV lines."

Embarrassed, Johnson said, "I'll go get coffee."

"Good idea, Mark. I'll take sugar and a little cream in mine." Then Paula said to the Doctor, "He's not my husband. We just work together."

"Oh. The way he stood by you in the ER, I just thought you were a couple. Sorry about that."

"No problem, Doc. So he was worried, huh?"

"Very much so," replied the Doctor. "Your ribs will be sore for a few days so take it easy. Otherwise, you're good to go. I'll tell the nurse to unplug you."

John C. LaBella

* * *

Paula was quiet and dozed off in the car on the way back home. When she woke she asked Johnson to describe the shooting. She had blanked out after she went down and didn't remember too much. He described all of the details as well as he could from memory. "Thanks, Mark. And thanks for getting me out of there and taking care of me. I won't forget it. But my poor car sounds totaled."

"Come on Paula, you would have done the same for me. We're partners – right?"

"Yes, Mark." Paula reflected for a moment. She thought about how Johnson was there for her a few days ago when the SFPD dumped her. And it was Johnson who, a few months earlier, helped her get back into homicide with the Farallones case. She turned to him and said softly, "We sure are..."

"Have you spoken to Jurek today?"

"No. I haven't. I'll call him when we get back into cell coverage again." The ride southbound was going well. The combination of tall evergreens and mountain peaks created a great view but hampered cell connections once again. An hour and a half later they drove through the town of Willits, California. Hungry, they stopped for a burger and a bio break at one of the fast food places on the main drag.

Hot! In Tomales

When Paula stepped out of the car Johnson saw that she was a little wobbly, she had a difficult time walking. Light-headed and disoriented, Paula held Johnson's arm to make sure she didn't fall. "Are you okay, Paula? It's a good time for a break."

"I'm fine Mark. Too much sitting, plus I haven't eaten much the past couple of days. I'll be okay in a minute."

"Will you need help in the bathroom or can you manage things on your own?"

"What the hell kind of a question is that? Look. I said I was fine."

Johnson waited outside the ladies restroom for Paula. She seemed ok as she walked out. Pointing to a booth near the window he said, "Maybe you can take a seat over there and save the table. I'll get the food. What can I get for you?"

"I'll take a double cheese, fries, and a...ah..."

"And a what, Paula?"

"A dead cot...no, no. A died, a rock...dede..." Paula was talking gibberish. She knew she wanted a diet cola but couldn't get the words out.

"Crap," Johnson said out loud. *She's having a stroke and I'm the only one here that can help her.*

The girl at the counter, waiting to take their order, was watching intently. She could see Paula struggling. Johnson asked her if she had an aspirin.

"You're in luck, sir." She handed him a couple of tablets and a cup of water.

"Thanks," he said to the girl as he gave the aspirin and water to Paula. From his first responder training he remembered that aspirin in the first few minutes of a stroke is crucial in order to minimize damage.

"Should I call the rescue squad?" asked the girl.

"Let's wait a minute to see how she does."

"Okay," she said, handing him the bag with their food order in it.

Within ten minutes Paula was better. "We need to get you back to Marin and checked out at the hospital." Paula knew something was wrong when Johnson said to her, "Look at me and smile."

"What? Are you nuts."

"Look at me and smile, damn it. I want to see if one side of your face is drooping more than the other." Her symmetry looked normal; a good sign.

"If you're still acting goofy when we get back to Marin, we're going straight to the ER."

"Sure, Mark. That's fine. Can I have my burger now?" Johnson shook his head in disbelief as he watched her eat. *Paula is returning to normal.*

Thirty minutes later, and back on the 101, she announced that they had cell coverage and called Jurek. "Where are you, Jurek?"

"Hi, Paula. I'm over in the C-Mart break-room matching register receipts of kerosene purchases with the video records from the registers."

"Any luck, yet?" asked Paula.

"Well sort of, I guess. I found two receipts for kerosene purchases in the two weeks preceding the fires. The video files have pictures of both buyers too. One is an older woman, I'd say in her sixties or seventies. The other is a male. His face was shaded by his hoodie making it difficult to see clearly."

"Did either of them pay with a credit card?"

"Nope. Both were cash customers."

"Ask C-Mart for copies of the two videos with the kerosene purchases on them. I want to get some still pictures of them."

"Tell Jurek we'll be back to headquarters later today, about three or so," whispered Johnson.

"Jurek, let's plan to meet at three thirty today in the squad room to go over what you have."

"Sounds good, Paula."

* * *

Traffic on the 101 was building, as they neared Marin. "This is odd," said Johnson, making small talk. "The southbound traffic is usually lighter in the afternoon but not today. How 'ya doin', Paula?"

"I'm fine. No need for the ER. Let's get to the squad room and take a look at our suspects."

"Okay, but you need to take it easy."

Jurek hadn't heard about the shooting. Reacting to her bandaged head when she walked in, he said. "Wow. What the hell happened to you?"

"We got jumped by some trigger happy assholes in the hills just south of Eureka," said Paula. "If you think *I'm* banged up, you should see my car."

"Paula, perhaps you should sit this out and let Jurek and I go over the transaction tapes."

"No way in hell. We're close to seeing a picture of our arsonist. I'm not 'sitting this out', Mark."

"So, I've noted the time stamps on the register tapes for the kerosene purchases and then found the cash register videos that matched those times."

"Jurek, are you sure that the registers and video cameras are in sync with each other and also with the actual time of day?" asked Johnson.

"Mark, they are. I spoke to, Woody, the head of C-Mart's video surveillance and theft prevention program. He said that each register has a unique identifier and its own dedicated camera too."

"But is the time of day on the register tapes and the time on the videos, in sync?" asked Chen.

"Yes," replied Jurek. "The time and date stamps are all synced up and tested daily. C-Mart uses the information from the registers and cameras to catch and prosecute shoplifters. There are two people who fit into our timeframe."

"Let's take a peek at those pictures," said Paula.

Jurek showed her enlarged printouts of the two people from the videos. "Hey. That's the woman who runs the store," said Paula when she saw the picture of the elderly woman. "I met her and spoke to her. I've got her name here in my notes...just a second...found it. Her name is Harriet Grant. She runs the Tomales general store."

"How many cans of kerosene did Grant buy?"

"She bought two cases, that's sixteen two-quart cans. Our mystery man bought eight."

"I don't think Grant is our arsonist," said Paula. "I'm betting she bought those cans as inventory to re-sell at the general store. I've got a feeling that the guy who bought eight cans is our man, four for each fire."

"It's not a great picture but we've got to show it to everyone in the Tomales area. Maybe someone will recognize the clothing," said Jurek.

"It's getting late. Let's meet in the morning to finalize our plans. Mark, maybe you can go house-to-house. Jurek, I'd like you to check with the local businesses; the deli, the store, the hotel..."

"Sure, Paula. Sounds good," said Jurek.

Johnson was reviewing the facts out loud. "Four two-quart cans of kerosene for each fire?"

"That's a lot of kerosene for the size of those structures. Plus, four cans is a lot of weight to carry too," said Jurek.

"Wait a minute, were you morons out sick the day they taught simple math? I thought there were three fires?"

"You're right, Paula," said Johnson.

"I found two of those two-quart cans at each of the fires I investigated," said Jurek. "That's a total of four. And don't forget about the first fire, the one where the building was razed because no body died in it. I'll bet two cans were used for that one too – so that makes a total of six."

"Shit," said Paula, "he bought eight cans and only used six so far. Does this mean there's gonna' be a fourth fire?"

Chapter 22

Paula had arrived early hoping to jump-start the day. "Good morning," she said when Johnson and Jurek entered the squad room. Paula was feeling better but Johnson still noticed that she had some trouble with her balance. That didn't stop her. She steadied herself by holding onto the frame of the whiteboard as she wrote her thoughts on it.

"I need a coffee before we get started. Can I get one for either of you?" Johnson asked pouring a cup from the grungy old pot that's been in a corner of the squad room for years. Chen and Jurek declined. "So, Paula," he went on, "Let's suppose you're right and there is a fourth fire looming, we need to figure out who the next victim will be."

"If we could do that," added Jurek. "We could stop the bastard before he sets his fourth fire."

"Right guys. When you two go to Tomales and walk the picture of our suspect around, door-to-door, maybe someone will recognize him."

"Paula, are sure you're ok staying here alone?"

"Mark, look, I'm fine. If I need help the whole damn building is full of cops. I'll work on making a list of knowledge gap questions while your gone. Maybe I can organize our thoughts a little..."

* * *

Slowed by yet another day of coastal fog and those winding roads, Jurek and Johnson arrived in Tomales at ten. By eleven-thirty Johnson had visited seven houses with no luck. His age was showing. He was exhausted but kept on task. At the eighth house he was greeted by an elderly woman, "Hello, Ma'am. Sorry to disturb you. I'm Detective Mark Johnson with the Marin County Sheriff's office." His badge was hung on the outside of his coat pocket in plain view. "May I ask you a few questions?"

"Yes, Detective. How can I help you?" asked the woman, a long time resident of Tomales.

"Have you seen this person?" asked Johnson as he showed her the picture of the man who had recently bought eight two-quart cans of kerosene at the C-Mart. He was expecting her to give him his eighth "no" but she surprised him.

"Why yes, Detective," said the old woman. "He looks familiar. What did you say your name was?"

"Mark Johnson. I'm Detective Mark Johnson. What's your name, Ma'am?"

"I'm Tilly Martinson. Won't you please come in?" As Johnson entered the house he was greeted with the raunchy smell of mothballs, old dust and incontinence. They stood in the living room as she went on, "I've lived in this house for over forty years you know."

"So what can you tell me about the man in the picture, Miss Martinson?"

"I'm sure he's the man I saw that night, the night when Gracie was killed. I guess our curiosity simply got the better of us as a small group had gathered across the street from the fire. All of a sudden, some guy wearing a dark hooded sweatshirt shoved past me from behind. It spun me around. But I got a pretty good look at his face."

"Did he hurt you, Ma'am?"

"No, he just rushed right past me. I lost my balance for a second or two...so rude. Never said excuse me or anything."

"I'm glad you weren't hurt. You said you got a good look at his face. Do you remember anything else like how tall he was or his age?"

"I'll try, Detective. He was younger, maybe in his thirties or forties. His hair was dark, probably brown or possibly even reddish-brown."

"Did he have a beard or a moustache?"

"No, he was clean shaven. His friend, however, he had a full white beard, like Santa's. He had the most sad soulful eyes I've ever seen."

"Wait. You say he had a friend with him? Take your time and please, try to relax. Is there anything else you remember about either of those men or about that night in general?"

"Let me see..." Tilly sat quietly, deep in thought for a moment. The clock on the wall between the living room and bedroom was ticking. The kitchen faucet was dripping into a pot in the sink. Then she looked at Johnson, "Yes. Yes there is. I thought it was odd that they were wearing dark clothing from head to toe, dark blue or black, hard to tell. It's not safe to dress in dark clothes at night you know."

"Can you tell me anything else about them?"

"Hmm," she said. "It was dark out. And, oh yes, how could I forget? The younger man, the one in the picture, he was wearing rubber boots. The kind we used to wear in the shucking room years ago."

"You worked in the shucking room? Was it at the Dream Bay Oyster Company?" asked Johnson.

"Why yes, Detective. How did you know that?"

"Just a lucky guess, Ma'am. So tell me what else you can remember about the man's friend, the guy with the white beard."

Hot! In Tomales

"Like I said, he was dressed in dark clothes too, from head to toe. They stood close to each other at first but didn't speak much. They just stood there watching the fire like the rest of us."

* * *

The Westward Inn of Tomales was built shortly after the massive earthquake of nineteen hundred and six. It resembled a western saloon with heavy shutters and it had a two-piece swinging front door inviting visitors into the lobby. It was the first stop for Jurek when he and Johnson arrived in Tomales.

A note hung on the door informed guests to *Please check-in after twelve-noon. The desk clerk comes on duty at that time.* The note also gave a phone number for people to call in case of emergency or if they needed an early check-in. Unfortunately, there were no payphones in Tomales and cell coverage was non-existent. Jurek could not call the number so he decided to return after noon to talk to the clerk at the inn.

While Johnson was going door-to-door, Jurek visited the Tomales Deli where he met the owners, Manuel Diego and his wife Sandi. Manuel explained that the Tomales saloon stood on the site before they bought the property. They converted it into the

Deli nine years ago. "I'm sorry, Senor," Diego said when Jurek showed him the picture, "I do not remember seeing anyone who looks like this man."

Jurek walked across the street to the Tomales General Store. It was one of those old-time places that stocked anything anyone might need. He asked the young girl behind the counter, no older than thirteen, if she had seen the man in the picture. She said, "No, sir. I haven't. Maybe you can come back tomorrow morning, early. My Grandma will be here then and she knows everyone."

Jurek left the general store shortly after twelve and walked back across the street to see if the desk clerk had arrived at the inn. As he entered, Molly Parker, a charming woman in her mid-forties, greeted him. "Good afternoon, Ma'am," he said. "I'm Jurek Grotowski with the Marin County Fire Service. I'm conducting an investigation to learn about a recent fire here in Tomales."

"Sure. How can I help?"

"I would like to know if you remember seeing this man?" asked Jurek, showing her the picture.

"Well, he sure does look familiar. I think he might have stayed with us a few weeks back...with a friend. It was about the time of that awful fire that killed Miss Loomis."

"Did he pay with a credit card?"

"No. I remember that he was a walk-in. The guests that make online reservations hold them with a credit card. Because we have such poor Internet connections in Tomales, walk-in guests usually have to pay with cash. It takes forever to get on the Internet to verify their cards."

"I was hoping I could get a name for this guy from his charge card record. Are you sure he's the same man you had as a guest?"

"It's hard to tell from the picture, but it seems to be the same man." She saw the disappointment on Jurek's face. "Wait a minute. Our policy is to ask for a photo ID when guests arrive. I took some information from his driver's license. Let me look through our register, it'll only take a minute."

"Thanks, Ma'am."

"Would you like a cup of coffee, Detective?"

"Oh, I'm not a detective, Ma'am. I'm an arson investigator. It would sure be great if you could look through that register. I'd appreciate it. And yes, I'd love a cup of coffee. Black thanks."

The small hotel had nine guest rooms and was a replica of the original Westward Inn that stood on this location since the late eighteen hundreds. Jurek was looking at old pictures that hung in the lobby as he waited for the desk clerk to search. There was a picture on the wall of the massive earthquake of nineteen hundred and six. That quake took down the original Inn and much of San Francisco. The fires in the city that followed the quake intrigued Jurek. *How did they fight fires like that back in the day?*

The "big quake" occurred in April of 1906 and most of San Francisco, everything east of Van Ness Street, was lost in the fire. However, the picture that captured Jurek's attention hung over an antique fainting couch. It was four gals dressed from head to toe in wet-gear – the type of outer clothes worn in shucking rooms. Intrigued, Jurek studied the picture. He was drawn to one of the faces that caught his attention. He studied it closely and then it struck him...he was looking at his grandmother.

The desk clerk came back to the lobby with a worried look on her face, "Somehow, that register has gone missing. I've no idea what might have happened to it."

Still locked on the picture, Jurek did not register what Molly told him. "Do you know the names of the women in this picture?" pointing to the picture of the four women. "This one sure looks like my grandmother."

"We call it, 'The Mother Shuckers.' You'll find their names are written on the back." Jurek took it off the wall, turned it over and sure enough, one of the names on the back of the picture was Juliana

Grotowski, his grandmother. The others were Tilly Martinson, Emily Donegras, and Grace Loomis.

Drawing attention back to Jurek's request, Molly said, "Detective, I'm so sorry. The register is always kept under the front counter, but it's gone. I have no idea what became of it."

"Wow. That's strange. Do you think you would be able to recognize the man's name if you heard it again?"

"I think so..."

"Was it Jimmy Loomis?" asked Jurek.

"No, no. I know Jimmy and it weren't him."

"How about Angus McGee?"

"No. I know Angus too...such a sweet boy."

"Jacobus McDermott?" Asked Jurek, referring to the names Chen and Johnson shared with him.

"No, Detective. I wish I could find my notes."

Jurek had decided that it was no use to correct the woman about his title. Then he offered the only other name he could remember from the discussion with Chen and Johnson.

"Was it Burke? Paddy Burke?"

"That's the name, Detective. I'm sure of it. Well, to be clear now, that's the name of the guy's friend. The one in your picture let the older guy, Burke, pay for the room. I took his information but I didn't ask any questions."

"Are you absolutely sure you recognize the man and could recognize his friend too?"

"Yes, I'm sure of it. It was Burke. I thought it was kind of odd how he spelled his first name." She pulled out a blank sheet of stationary paper from the desk. "He wrote it out like this, *P a d r a i c,* but he pronounced it *Paddy.*"

"Do you recall what he looked like? Can you describe his face at all? Hair color, whiskers, bald, full head of hair?"

"Yes. He looked old with a full white beard. He was bald on top with a ponytail hanging down from the back of his head – his hair was snow white too."

"This is very helpful, Ma'am. Thank you."

"One other thing, Detective; the guy didn't look at all like the picture on his license."

"Go on..."

"The picture on his license looked like that radio talk show fella, Rush ahhh, what's-his-name? I asked him why he didn't look like the picture on his license. He told me it was a very old picture."

"Did you happen to notice the expiration date on his license?" asked Jurek.

"Yes, in fact I wrote it down. Say, now that you got me thinking about it, his license was not due to expire for three more years."

"That means the picture was two years old."

"Like I said, it didn't make sense to me that it was an old picture."

"Right, California requires that a driver's license is renewed every five years. And a new picture is taken when it's renewed. Is there anything else you remember about this man?"

"Well, his partner, the one in that picture of yours, seemed to be way too young for him."

"Too young?"

"Well, yes, a lot younger. The two of them acted like they'd been together for quite a few years. The way they spoke to each other reminded me of an old married couple. Plus they dressed alike too. They were both wearing dark clothing and looked like cat burglars. That younger man was wearing rubber boots though...not sure why."

Chapter 23

"So, what'd you learn?" Johnson asked when they met back at the car on Main Street.

"Got some good info, Mark. The innkeeper said our boy spent the night of the fire at the inn."

"I'll call Paula and set up time to meet with her when we get back. By the way, I got lucky too."

"Jeez...that just doesn't sound like you Mark."

"Right. What I meant was that I met a woman, Tilly Martinson who said that she had remembered seeing our guy the night of the fire. She also said there was another man with him."

"Mark, that confirms the desk clerk's story. She recognized our guy and told me he was with another man. We'll look through the crowd pictures I have from the night of the fire, back at the station."

"Any luck at the Deli or General Store?"

"Even though the man in the picture stayed at the hotel the night of the fire, nobody at the Deli or General Store recalled seeing him."

"No reason to hang around after setting the fire. He probably left later that night or next morning."

"And, there's more. I was looking at some old photos in the lobby of the hotel. And, Mark, guess who I recognized in one of them?"

"Mother Teresa? I give up. Who?"

"My grandmother..."

* * *

Johnson and Jurek walked into the squad room to find Paula at the whiteboard. Jurek told her about his interview with the hotel clerk who told him the guy in the picture had a partner – an older man.

Johnson said, "I spoke to Tilly Martinson. She remembered our guy plus a second man as well."

"Slow down guys, I want to make sure I capture all of this on the board." After a minute she was caught up. "OK, What else?"

"I saw a picture of four women all dressed in shucking gear on the wall in the hotel lobby," said Jurek. "It turns out that my grandmother, Juliana Grotowski, was in the picture along with Grace Loomis, Emily Donegras and Tilly Martinson. That proves that the four women knew each other and that they probably worked together. I wonder how close they were? Do they hold a shared secret?"

"Is it possible that one of them might be victim number three?" asked Johnson.

"Good questions," said Chen. "We can assume from the picture that they all knew each other. I'm betting that the motive will likely include all of them. I'll put a call into Jonah. He may be able to help us determine the motive." Paula picked up the phone and called Jonah to see if he was free to join them.

"Let's recap," said Jurek. "Two of the women in the picture of four are dead. The third still lives in Tomales, a short distance from the fires. The fourth one, my grandmother, is in an assisted living facility a mile or so outside of San Rafael," Doctor Chiang entered the squad room as he said this.

"Hi, everyone," said Chiang. "Jurek, do you guys happen to have the full names of the two women that are still living? The one in Tomales and your grandmother, Jurek?"

"Yes," said Johnson. "Her first name is Tilly, I guess it's short for Matilda, last name Martinson."

"And my grandmother's full name is Juliana Grotowski."

"Ok, I'll be back in a half hour," said Chiang. "I want to run those names through the Greater Bay Area Cancer Registry (GBACR) to see if they have been diagnosed with a cancer that is similar to what Loomis and Donegras had. Later."

"Go for it Jonah," said Chen. "That information could be key in helping us establish a motive."

"Here's something else guys," said Jurek. "The clerk at the hotel said that for some reason, the guest registry was missing. I ran a few names by her and she connected on one of them. It was Paddy Burke and he..."

"Are you serious? Why in the hell didn't you mention that before? Paddy Burke is one of the men who founded La Ostra, LLC. That's the group that owned all of the burned buildings," Johnson said.

"I heard you mention his name when you and Paula returned from Eureka. I guess I didn't realize the connection," said Jurek. "Sorry about that."

"What else did the clerk at the inn have to say about Burke?" asked Paula.

"She told me that he didn't look anything at all like the picture on his driver's license. She told me that the man who checked in was older, with a full beard, snow-white hair, and..." before Jurek could finish, Johnson jumped in.

"Sounds like McDermott. I bet the man she had described ain't Burke at all, it's Jacko McDermott."

"Mark, you and Frasier found Burke dead on his cabin floor? Correct? Heart attack, right?"

"Yes," said Johnson. "And maybe his death was more than a coincidence. Now I'm thinking that he may have been murdered. I'm going back up to Eureka tomorrow morning to review the case with the Humboldt County Medical Examiner. I have a few questions for Detective Frasier too."

"Mark, I'm not sure I can make that trip with you right now," said Paula. "I guess I'm still feeling a little weak and somewhat unstable. Jurek, can you go along with him?"

"I can handle it alone, Paula," replied Johnson. "Jurek needs to get back to the clerk at the inn with a photo of McDermott. Hopefully the clerk will validate that he was the man who checked in using Burke's name."

"Who's got a recent picture?" asked Jurek.

"I have one on my phone, I also have a picture of Burke too – a still picture of him lying dead on the floor. I'll send them to you right now."

"Jurek, when you to go back to Tomales, I want you to show them to Tilly Martinson too."

"Sure, no problem, Paula. I'll leave as soon as I can print the pictures that Mark is sending."

"Hey, guys. Got a minute?" it was Chiang.

"Sure, did you find anything?" asked Paula.

"The database has a file on Matilda Martinson. I'm afraid I've got bad news...she has cancer too, a similar form to the one that Loomis and Donegras were suffering from."

"What about my grandmother?" Jurek asked.

"She didn't show up on the database. Now, it doesn't mean she doesn't have cancer, it just means she's not being treated for it," said Chiang.

"OK. Thanks. I guess," said Jurek. "She seems to be as healthy as ever except for her memory. And I don't think she's taking any medications. Plus, nothing seems to be physically wrong with her."

"Good signs, Jurek. Individuals react differently to carcinogenic stimuli," Chiang said. "Even though she may have been exposed to the identical radiation as the others, there are other factors that could have created a different outcome for her."

"Thanks, Doc," said Jurek. His phone buzzed indicating a new message. It was the pictures from Johnson. "I'll print these and head out to Tomales shortly. When I get back, I'll run a photo of the guy who bought the kerosene through our new facial recognition software. Maybe we'll get lucky."

"Say, Jonah. Is it possible to run a toxicology screen from our two fire scenes?"

"Sure, Mark" replied Chiang. "Why do you ask? The two women died from complications resulting from the fires. It's pretty much cut and dried."

"Humor me for a minute," said Johnson. "What if the killer did not want them to suffer – or at least wanted them to be numb to the pain?"

"An arsonist with a heart?" asked Chen. "Do you really think that's the case, Mark?"

"Maybe he wanted to give them some sort of a sedative so they wouldn't be able to escape – or hear someone, such as the arsonist, enter the house?"

"That may make sense, Mark," said Jurek. "The first victim, Emily Donegras never got out of bed."

"Yes, that's true," said Chiang. "But our autopsy showed that she died from a heart attack."

"What if that heart attacked was caused by some sort of an external stimuli?" asked Johnson.

"I suppose it's possible, Mark. We didn't find much at the scene, just some pills. I think they were lorazepam to help with nausea from the chemo."

"Jurek, was there anything else at the scene that may have been used to sedate them?" asked Chen.

"I remember seeing oyster shells at the Loomis fire, maybe they were tainted, and teacups. Maybe there was something in the tea," said Jurek. "But the cups were empty by the time I got there."

"Mark, if you feel strongly about this, we can run a screen on the oyster shells," said Chiang.

"And the teacups?" asked Johnson.

"You really seem to be hung up on the teacups, Mark. Tell us what you're thinking," said Chen.

"I da' know. There were some teacups sitting on the table in Burke's cabin too. In fact, they'd been there so long that the contents had evaporated. Burke did not appear to have any risk factors for heart disease. However, all the signs indicated that he died from acute heart failure."

"Sure, Mark. We can use distilled water to titrate residual compounds in the teacups from the Loomis fire. It should take a couple of days if it's a common poison; longer if it's a rare substance."

"Thanks, Jonah. Give me a call if you find something. I'll call Frasier and Doctor James to let them know I'll be up there tomorrow."

"Mark," asked Chiang, "Do you want me to call Doctor James to compare my findings to hers?"

"Sure, Jonah, good idea. Thanks."

"I think we need to cut Jimmy lose, guys," said Paula. "We simply don't have enough to hold him."

"I agree," said Johnson. "See you soon..."

"OK, Mark. Be careful, especially in the woods."

"Right, Paula. No kidding. I'm planning to stay one night and be back in town late in the afternoon on the day after tomorrow. I'll brief you with what I find then."

Johnson called Frasier and arranged a meet with him at eleven o'clock the next morning. Unable to reach Doctor James, he left a message that he would see her later that day, between two and three.

Chapter 24

Jurek wanted to make sure the two women in Tomales would be available before driving out there. He called the desk clerk at the inn first. When she answered, he knew she had been asleep.

"Hello..." a groggy voice, still in sleep mode, answered. "Hello...this is Molly, who's calling?"

"Molly, sorry to wake you, Ma'am. This is Jurek Grotowski, I spoke with you yesterday about the fire that killed Grace Loomis."

"Yes, Detective...how can I help you?"

"I would like to meet with you later to show you another picture. Is nine thirty ok?"

"Let's see...what's the time right now?" she said, looking at her clock. "Holy cow, it's only seven... sure, I guess I could meet you at nine thirty."

"Thanks, Molly. Sorry for waking you. I'll see you at nine thirty at the inn." Next he called Tilly Martinson. "Miss Martinson?"

"Yes, this is Tilly Martinson. Who's calling?"

Hot! In Tomales

"This is Jurek Grotowski with the Marin County Fire service. Detective Mark Johnson spoke with you yesterday about the recent fire. He said that you recognized someone in a picture he showed you."

"He's such a nice young man."

"He is, Miss Martinson. I have another picture I'd like to show you. Is nine too early for you?"

"Nine o'clock today? No. That should be fine."

"Thank you, Ma'am. I'll see you soon."

* * *

Jurek knocked on Tilly Martinson's door at precisely nine o'clock. "Hello, Miss Martinson, I'm Jurek Grotowski. Thank you for meeting with me on short notice. I have another picture to show you regarding the fire at the Loomis house."

"Sure, Detective. Won't you come in?"

"Does this man look familiar, Miss Martinson?"

Tilly stood there for a moment, deep in thought, like she was in a trance. "Grotowski?" she repeated his name. "Are you related to Julie Grotowski?"

Surprised by the question, Jurek said proudly, "Yes. Juliana Grotowski is my grandmother."

"Oh. I knew Julie. We worked in the shucking room together for years. She's such a sweet lady." Then, a moment later, she shifted to the picture of

Jacko McDermott. "Yes, he sure does. He was in the crowd at the fire along with that other fella."

Jurek was having a difficult time following her as she flitted from topic to topic. Then he showed her the picture of Burke. "What about this guy? Miss Martinson, do you remember seeing him on the night of the fire?"

"Oh my. He looks awful. I've never seen him."

"Are you sure? Take another look."

"I'm sure. I've never seen this man before."

"Thank you for your time Ma'am."

* * *

Jurek drove two blocks to the inn. He parked on a side street running downhill along the building. A light rain was falling as he made his way under the overhang to the lobby. Molly was waiting to let him in. "Good morning, Molly. Thanks for seeing me. Can you take a look at this picture and tell me if this man looks familiar?"

"Oh my god," Molly said. "That's him. That's the man. He's the one who introduced himself as Paddy Burke. I'm sure of it."

"Thank you, Molly. I have just one more picture for you. Do you recall seeing this man?" Jurek showed her a picture of the real Paddy Burke.

She studied the picture for a minute and said, "No. Never saw him. He doesn't look at all well."

"The picture was taken after he was found dead on the floor of his cabin. Sorry if it upset you."

"Oh, man. So the other guy, the old fart who checked in using Burke's ID...what's his name?"

Jurek knew he could not discuss case details. Rudely, he said, "Thank you for your time, Molly."

* * *

Recently certified in the newer, 3D version of facial recognition software, Jurek was anxious to get back to the squad room. He wanted to run profiles on the picture of the man who purchased those cans of kerosene at the C-Mart. The newer version did a better job of both recognizing and mapping facial contours. It was able to provide stronger matches against known samples, a definite improvement over the old 2D software. It was especially useful with pictures taken in low-light conditions.

"Jurek," said Chen as she walked into the squad room. "How was your trip to Tomales?"

"Valuable, Paula. Both Molly Parker and Tilly Martinson recalled seeing Jacko McDermott on the night of the fire. But neither recognized the picture of Paddy Burke. Molly Parker, the hotel clerk, also confirmed that it was McDermott who presented Burke's driver's license as his own."

"Good work. We have new gaps," said Paula as she began to write them on the white board. "Did McDermott kill the women? Why did he want them dead? Did he act alone? If not, who helped him?"

"Hopefully we'll be able to answer all of those questions soon, Paula. I scanned the picture of the man from C-Mart, the one who bought eight cans of kerosene, into our new version of the facial recognition software. I came up empty on the first pass. But when I ran it a second time I got a hit."

"And the winner is...?"

"Milford Neville."

"Common, you're kidding me? Milford Neville? That name sounds like it's right of out of a Doctor Seuss book. Does he have any priors?"

"He's young, only thirty five, but he's been busted three times for arson. His latest arrest landed him a five year sentence, but he was out after two years for good behavior."

"Does the database tell us anything regarding his methods or current whereabouts?"

"Still digging, should have it in a minute."

"OK, call me when you find something. I'm going down to the lab to see if Jonah has any new news for us."

"Wait a minute, Paula. Here it is now. His last known address was in one of those communes up in Humboldt County."

"Probably one of the pot farms – or should I say a cannabis cultivation operation?"

"It goes on to say that his last two fires used trailers to set up multi-stage events. The accelerant in all three fires was..."

"Let me guess. Kerosene?"

"Right. Kerosene. And the burn trailers he uses are his trademark."

"Let's see if we can get in touch with Mark. We should let him know what you've found regarding McDermott and his involvement with," she said with a snicker, "Mister Milford Neville."

Johnson was just about to walk into the Humboldt County Sheriff's office when she reached him. "Mark, we've got a couple of developments that you should probably know about."

"Hey, Paula. Whatcha' got?"

"Just a sec, let me put Jurek on to explain it."

"Hi, Mark. For starters, both of the witnesses in Tomales recognized Jacko McDermott as the man they remembered seeing the night of the fire. McDermott is also identified as the one who had checked into the inn using Burke's ID."

"Wow, that's a big break, Jurek."

"Right. We also have a name for the guy who purchased the kerosene at the C-Mart. His name is Milford Neville."

"Are you shitting me?"

"No, Mark," replied Chen. She couldn't hold it back any longer and broke into a laugh. "That's his real name."

"His last known address is a commune up in Humboldt County," said Jurek.

"This is really good stuff to know, thanks. I've got a meeting scheduled with Detective Frasier in a few minutes. After that, I'm meeting with Doctor Jillian James, the ME, this afternoon."

"Should we ask Jonah to be available when you meet with Doctor James? It's your call, Mark."

"That's a good idea, Paula. Tell him I'll call if the conversation goes too medical for me."

"Great. Let us know what you find," said Chen. "And be careful."

"I plan to drive back home later today. I'll call you from the car to give you a briefing about my meetings today; probably be after dinner." Johnson said as he approached an old building with a limestone façade. "Humboldt County Sheriff" was chiseled into the stone above the pillars.

"Can I help you, sir?" asked the young man at the front desk in the Sheriff's Office.

"Yes. I'm Detective Mark Johnson from Marin County. I have a meeting with Detective Frasier at eleven thirty. I guess I'm a little early. I can wait if he's tied up right now."

"Let me check."

"Thanks." Johnson was nervous and couldn't stop fidgeting with the zipper on his jacket.

"You're in luck, Detective Johnson. He'll see you right now." Johnson entered Frasier's office.

Frasier got up from behind his desk to shake Johnson's hand. "Detective Johnson, good to see you again. How is your partner, Patty Chen, doing?"

"It's Paula, not Patty, and she's doing much better. Thanks for asking."

"Give her my best. So tell me, Detective, what brings you back to Eureka?"

"I'm here to question Jacko McDermott. I have reason to believe that he and another man are behind the fires down in Tomales."

"That's a pretty strong statement, Johnson. Tell me why you think Mister McDermott is involved in those fires."

"For starters, two eye witnesses saw him in Tomales on the night of the fire on December fifth. We also have crime scene photos of him watching the fire from across the street. Plus, he booked a room at the local hotel that same evening."

"Pretty circumstantial evidence, Detective. So he was in Tomales? So What? Did anyone see him light the fire or throw gasoline on it?"

"No. The only person that could have seen him doing those things is dead."

"So, tell me again. Why do you want to bother Jacko McDermott?"

"He checked into the Westward Inn as Paddy Burke and used Burke's driver's license for ID."

"But we found Burke's ID on him, when the autopsy was performed."

Johnson was getting angry. "I'm only asking you once. Do you want to be present when I question McDermott or should I go find him on my own?"

"Now calm down, Detective. I'll be happy to take you to his cabin. Are you ready to go?"

"Yes. The sooner the better." The two men got into Frasier's black Crown Vic cruiser and headed out to the commune.

When they arrived at McDermott's door, Frasier knocked loudly. "Jacko, come on out and talk to us. It's the sheriff. We need your help with something, Jacko. If you're in there, come out now."

"Go away," replied a grumpy voice inside of the cabin. "Come back with some paper..."

"Listen, Jacko. Being a hard-ass ain't gonna' help your case. It makes you look guilty."

"I am guilty, Frasier. I killed those women down in Tomales and I killed Burke too. There. Are ya' happy now? You've got your confession."

Surprised to hear this admission, Johnson said, "Let's talk about it Jacko. Why would you want to kill them? What was your motive."

"Kill who?" asked McDermott.

"The two women in Tomales and Burke," said Johnson. "You just confessed to killing them."

"Well guess what, you never bothered to read me my rights, Detective. So that means my entire confession ain't admissible in court. Now get the hell off my property."

"I suppose he's right. We better leave. Nothing he admitted can be used in a trial."

"That's bullshit, Frasier, and you know it. We never placed him in custody nor detained him. So anything he says before *that* point, even without reading him his Miranda rights, *is* admissible."

"I da' know. If he's guilty we don't want the case thrown out on a technicality."

"Look, Frasier. I have no idea why you're protecting him like you are. I'm going to cuff him, arrest him and take him in for ques..."

Before he could finish his sentence, the lights went out for Johnson.

Chapter 25

"Wake up damn it," she was frantic. Kneeling over his body she found a very weak heartbeat and a faint pulse. "Wake up."

Slowly, Johnson came to. He was lying on his side in the fetal position. "Where am I?" The room looked strange. He had no idea where he was or how he got there. He felt a lump on the back of his head – very sensitive. "What in the hell did you do to me? It really hurts."

"Lie still. I'll see if there's ice in the fridge." She poked around the freezer and found an old clump of cubes that had melted together. She placed it on a towel, stepped on it to break it up as best she could and smashed it on the floor. A few seconds later he passed out again; he was turning blue. "Oh my God. Stay with me," she pleaded. Determined to save his life, she cleared a space on the floor, rolled him onto his back and began giving him mouth-to-mouth along with chest compressions.

Johnson sputtered a minute or so later. He was breathing on his own but was disoriented. "What the...?" *Why is this woman kissing me?* He managed to push her off saying, "Stop it. I'm married. I can't let you to do this to me."

"For Christ's sake, Detective. Don't be an ass. I'm trying to save your life. Believe me, I had no choice but I took an oath, I'm a doctor." She calmed herself for a moment. "I came here to meet with you and Frasier. When I got here I found you passed out on the floor turning blue, you were not breathing."

Slowly regaining his wits Johnson said, "Wait a minute, you're Frasier's Doctor. Jamie something or other, right?"

"Close. I'm Doctor Jillian James. We met a few days ago in Paddy Burke's cabin when you and Detective Frasier found his body."

"Sure, I remember. It's fuzzy, but coming back."

"I'm concerned about the whack to the back of your head – it could be a skull fracture. We need to get you to the ER. Oh, and please call me JJ."

"So, Doctor JJ. Why are you here?"

"I heard you were coming out here with Frasier, to take down McDermott. That's a really bad idea, Detective. You don't know what you're up against."

"OK. But that doesn't explain why you're here."

"Frasier's a bad cop. We suspect that he's been in the pocket of the cannabis cultivators for some time. Weed is a big business around here."

Johnson interrupted her in the middle of her story, "How long have I been out, JJ?"

"Four or five hours. I was expecting you three hours ago. I called Frasier's office and Maggie told me that you two had driven out to see McDermott."

With JJ's help, Johnson stood up and tried to walk out to her car. He was dizzy and still reeling from the blow to his head. "Boy, this knot on the back of my head is really throbbing."

"It figures. Let's get you to an ER. Put your arm around my shoulder. I'll help you into my car."

Johnson began staggering. He was too large for JJ to support. "Whoa. I gotta' stop. I'm getting really dizzy." The dizziness was severe. Everything was spinning, even the shrubs planted around the cabin. Johnson couldn't help it and tossed his cookies as JJ struggled to get him to her car.

"That's to be expected with head trauma, its normal," she said, trying to reassure him.

"Thanks – is it OK if I call you JJ?"

"Sure, if you want," JJ had already told him he could call her JJ. *His memory is failing.*

"I don't think I'll be able to drive home today. I should call my wife and let her know where I am."

"Let's wait to call until we know the extent of your injuries. No sense in worrying her just yet."

On the drive back to Eureka Johnson asked JJ about the red flowering bushes along the highway. "They sure are beautiful," he said, forgetting he had asked Frasier about them.

"Funny you should ask, Detective. They are oleander bushes and the plant contains a substance called oleandrin, a poison. We found traces of it in Burke's tissue samples along with a residue of it in the teacups from his cabin."

"So wait a minute, JJ. Slow down please. You're saying Burke was poisoned? But it looked like he had a heart attack."

"Oleandrin poisoning gives the appearance of a heart event but it doesn't show up in the initial array of toxicology screens. Without doing a specific test for it, coroners often miss it."

"The coroner sees an apparent heart attack, and doesn't look further – especially in older victims?"

"Exactly. The perfect crime...almost."

"I have to call the ME in Marin County," he said, reaching for his phone. "Shit, I think my phone fell out in McDermott's cabin."

"I picked it up for you, it's in my bag."

"Thanks. You're making quite the impression on me today, JJ."

"No worries," she said softly. She wanted to keep him calm. After parking the car at the ER she reached into the back seat for Johnson's phone. As she reached, her body brushed across his shoulder. She was soft. She smelled good too. His imagination shifted into overdrive. "Here you go," she said as she handed him his phone.

Trying to change his train of thought he said, "So, the teacups tested positive for oleander too?"

"It's oleandrin. And yes, whoever wanted Burke dead, gave him a tea brewed with oleander leaves." Johnson took his phone and called Chen.

"Paula, I'm in Eureka with a skull fracture."

"Slow down, Mark. What in the hell are you talking about?"

"I was out questioning McDermott when I was hit on the back of the head with something heavy. I was out cold for several hours before Doctor James found me."

"Mark, if you die, Chao's gonna' kill you, and she'll never forgive me. Have you called her yet?"

"I will as soon as I get out of the ER. I'm calling to tell you that Burke was murdered. It was not a heart attack at all...he was poisoned."

"How do you know this, Mark?"

"Doctor James, JJ, found me passed out on the cabin floor. She got me breathing again."

"But how do you know Burke was poisoned?"

"JJ told me that she ran a test for a poison that comes from oleander bushes. It's called Oleandrin. It makes it look like the victim had a heart attack."

"Mark, what does this have to do with the fires in Tomales?"

"I have a hunch that both of the victims in the Tomales fires were given something in their tea. It's possible that it was oleander leaves."

"Thus, your fixation on the teacups... That's a great hunch, Mark. How do we know for sure?"

"Jonah's lab just needs to run a toxicology test for oleandrin. It doesn't show in the initial tox panels. I tried calling him but he's not at his desk. Can you track him down and ask him to test the fire victim's tissue for oleandrin poisoning?"

"Sure, I'll follow up with him."

"Thanks, Paula. Please ask him to check for any residuals in the teacups found at the fire scenes too. The cause of death for Donegras was listed as a heart attack, but it could have been caused by tea made with oleander leaves."

"But Loomis died as a result of the fires."

"Sure, but if she was given tea made with oleandrin, it may have impaired her thinking to the extent that she couldn't get out of the house. See if he can lift prints off the teacups too."

"This is a major break. Good job, Mark."

"Thanks, Paula. I've gotta' hang up. The ER doc is here to explain the extent of my injuries."

"Don't forget to call Chao."

* * *

"You're fortunate, Detective. I would have bet the farm that you had a skull fracture," said Doctor James as the two drove away from the hospital.

"Can you suggest a place to stay for the night? There's no way I'll be able to drive home tonight, JJ." After a pause he said, "Please call me Mark."

"Let's try the Best Western. It's clean and close by. It's only a few blocks from here."

"Can you drive me? If you don't have any plans for the evening, maybe we could discuss the case over dinner?"

"What about your car, Mark?"

"I'll get the car tomorrow morning."

"Sure, Detective...I mean, Mark. Dinner tonight works for me. Which case do you want to discuss?"

"JJ, you told me that Frasier was the target of some sort of investigation, right?"

"Yes, he became chummy with the pot growers. I'm on a taskforce looking into the huge pay-o-la's he's received from them. Big money."

"Lets find a place for dinner so we can go over the entire story. Marin County will pick up the tab."

"In that case there's a great steakhouse on the waterfront fifty yards behind the Best Western. Is that OK with you, Mark?"

"Sounds good to me."

At the table, JJ continued telling the story about how La Ostra, LLC saved the local crabbing fleet. "The crab business had become decimated by the economy. Burke and McDermott used the La Ostra, LLC to convert the fleet from crabbing to oyster farming. Their success resulted in the two of them becoming well connected with local political figures including the mayor, police chief, alders, and a bunch of folks with money."

"Something from the bar, Miss?"

"I'll have a rusty nail," JJ said to the waiter.

"And you sir?"

Johnson had been sober for a couple of months but he really wanted a drink. He thought about it but then relented. "I'll have a Diet Coke, with a wedge of lime."

"How long have you been sober, Mark?"

"What are you talking about, JJ?"

"Mark, there's nothing wrong with being on the wagon. The problems start when you fall off. My first husband was an alcoholic but never admitted it.

He died in a freakish diving accident seven years ago – too damn drunk to handle the dive-gear."

"I'm sorry to hear that, JJ." Then, his eyes met hers, "I've been a drunk all my life but I had been sober for twenty years thanks to my wife, Chao."

"She sounds like an amazing woman, Mark."

"Shit. I forgot to call her after the ER visit. It's too late now."

"But, Mark. Won't she be worried that you didn't come home?"

"She'll be upset if I call her and wake her too. I'll call in the morning."

"I hope she understands."

"She'll be fine. Let's get back to what you were telling me about Burke and McDermott. Look, Frasier already told me about how the La Ostra, LLC saved the oyster business. It's a great story but I'm more interested in what went wrong."

"Greed, Detective."

"JJ, come on, I told you to call me, Mark."

"Sorry, Mark. Greed. It always takes over and it always wins. Weed became legal for medical use back in ninety-six when Prop Two-Fifteen passed."

"We were talking about the oyster business but now you've shifted to medical marijuana."

"Sorry. I skipped ahead. Burke and McDermott made a ton of money off cannabis cultivation after it became legal. Later, that money was used to fund the oyster business."

"OK, got it. I'm following you now."

"The climate around Eureka is ideal for growing weed. It grows like, well, it grows like a weed."

"I thought Prop Two-Fifteen allowed just five plants per person. How can five plants translate into big money? Sounds like small potatoes to me, JJ."

"Communes were the answer. They sprang up across the countryside with two to three hundred people living in each commune. McDermott and Burke had lived in one too. Those communes, in the hills of Humboldt and Mendocino Counties, had morphed into pot growing co-ops. The co-ops were able to grow a lot of weed but had a difficult time getting it to market efficiently."

"But JJ, isn't it illegal to sell weed in the State of California? Explain the money flow for me?"

"It is illegal, at least for now, unless it's sold by a medical dispensary with a permit. Prop Two-Fifteen paved the way for it. The communes, or co-ops as they are called now, allowed up to three hundred members. Technically every person in the co-op was allowed five plants – that's a total of fifteen hundred plants for a three hundred person commune."

"Wow – that is a lot of pot, JJ. I'm surprised it isn't regulated."

"It's impossible to regulate, Mark. No one in the Sheriff's Office had time to count noses to verify the number of people in the commune. That meant they didn't know the exact number of pot plants on those co-op farms either. The business grew fast."

"What role did Burke and McDermott play?"

"They began by working with multiple co-ops to help them become more efficient at moving the weed to the medical dispensaries across the state."

"So they were in it from the beginning?"

"They were, and they made a fortune. They used the money to fund La Ostra, LLC."

"Help me JJ. Maybe it's that knock on my head, but if it's ok to grow and sell pot through a medical dispensary, what was Frasier's role?"

"It's a complicated mess, legally I mean, to grow and sell pot in California. Selling weed is still illegal at the Federal level. Since the banks are regulated by the feds the money generated by pot sales cannot be deposited into the U.S. banking system."

"So without checking accounts and credit cards the entire business runs on a giant pile of cash."

"Right. Frasier's role was to protect the cash. He built an armed security force to do just that and made a bundle off the growers and dispensaries."

"And the county allowed him do this? Didn't they see a conflict of interest?"

"The county relied on him and his guards to deter violent crime and keep the peace. However, the guys he hired were huge, well armed and mean. It didn't take long for them to become a strong-armed force of bullies."

"So far, what you've told me sounds legit. What was it that made him a 'bad cop'?"

"The oyster business."

"Come on, JJ. Now I'm really confused."

She put her hand on his forearm. Rubbing it gently while looking into his eyes she said, "He was the front man for La Ostra, Mark. They used him to bribe the National Park Service."

"To do what?"

"He bribed them so they would shut down all of the oyster farming in the Tomales Bay region. That was done to eliminate major competition."

"How in the hell did he pull that off?"

"Most of the original Tomales Bay oyster farms, with the exception of one, were built on lands that had originally been leased from the National Park Service in the eighteen-hundreds. Frasier bribed the Park Service into not renewing any of the Tomales Bay leases thereby killing the oyster business. Today, the Tomales Bay shoreline has been reverted back to being part of a great big National Park – with that one major exception."

"What's the major exception?"

"The Dream Bay Oyster Company."

"Interesting... So why did La Ostra buy homes in Tomales? Was Frasier creating a smoke screen?"

"I'm not sure, Mark. Perhaps..." She caught him gazing at her. She moved down his forearm and held his hand, "If La Ostra owned the homes, then maybe he figured the LLC would not be a suspect."

"So, do you believe Burke and McDermott were behind the fires in Tomales?"

"Yes," she was slurring her words a bit. When the waiter returned she said, "Another rusty please; and I'll have the rack of lamb – medium rare."

"Right away, Ma'am," he replied. "And what can I bring for you, sir?"

"A rib eye, medium with a side of mushrooms. I'll have a Jameson on the rocks. Make it a double."

* * *

The two of them drank more than they should have and closed the bar late that night. A breeze and light fog had moved in off of Humboldt Bay. "Let me help you back to your room, Mark." JJ held his arm as they stumbled back to the hotel and into the hallway leading to his room. Johnson had trouble with the room key and JJ snatched it from his hand.

Then she playfully nudged him out of the way and put the key into the slot.

Johnson was not brain-dead. He knew what JJ wanted. Then, rather impulsively, he put his arms around her and they began kissing. Leaning against the door they grabbed at each other's clothes. They were too drunk to realize what was happening when the door suddenly flew open. Still entwined in each other's arms they fell into the room and lay there, sprawled out on the floor, laughing. Their lips found each other again. Johnson wanted her. She wanted him. She kissed him deep and slow using her tongue in a way he had never experienced. He kissed her neck and began nibbling up to her ears. He reached for her and she for him. They were twisted up in each other's business and ready for more when suddenly Johnson said, "JJ, I think you better go."

"But, Marky. I'm too drunk to drive home."

Thinking with his other brain, the little one, he said, "Then maybe you should stay." At that very moment, right after he said it, he regretted it. *Now what?* Then he heard a familiar voice. It was coming from his phone.

"Mark, are you there? Hello. Hello?" It was Chao, frantically trying to reach him.

Chapter 26

Johnson called Chao's cell in a panic. "Chao? Sorry I think I butt-dialed you by mistake." With the phone covered he mouthed to JJ, "It's my wife..."

"Are you ok?" Chao asked. "It sounded like you were in some sort of a struggle."

"No, I mean yes, Chao. I'm fine."

"Where are you and how much did you drink?"

"Come on, Chao. I told you I was going to Eureka on business. I got jumped and ended up in the ER with a possible skull fracture. The meds are making me drowsy so I couldn't drive home today."

"Really?" Chao knew he was lying. She always knew when he was lying. "So, you're sleeping in the car like some sort of homeless person?"

"No. I'm in a hotel room."

"How did you get to a hotel if you can't drive? In case you're too drugged, or drunk, to read a clock, it's midnight. By the way, who's the woman?"

"The ER doctor. Her name is Jillian Jones."

"Jillian *Who*?"

"I mean James. Wanna' talk to her, Chao?"

"Yes. Put 'Miss James' on, Mark. I want to ask the little tramp if she makes a habit of doing house calls for all her patients, or is she giving you some sort of special of treatment?"

"OK, Chao. I'll put her on," said Johnson as he handed the phone to JJ.

"Hello," said JJ. "This is Doctor James..."

"Stay...Away...From...My...Man," said Chao.

"I think you have the wrong impression. Mark and I are working on a case together."

"Right. Let me say it another way – its sounds like you two were working on a case alright, a case of Jameson." Chao was angry. Not so much because of the woman in his room but because he had blown his sobriety. "If you don't leave right now, I'll hunt you down and cut you so bad you'll never be called *'Miss'* James again. Now get your F-ing ass away from my F-ing husband." Chao ended the call.

"Ahh – I better leave, Mark. She's really pissed."

"She gets that way at times."

"I can't blame her. You came up here, blew your sobriety and dragged me into your room."

"Right. I'm the bad guy and you're blameless?"

"Mark, listen," JJ said as they struggled to their feet. She was standing in front of him. Close enough

247

for him to breathe in the stale smell of Scotch and Drambuie on her breath. "You're a good-looking guy, and I'll admit that I was...well I actually still am, attracted to you. I'm sorry."

Johnson was melting in the heat of the moment. He tried to think of something witty to say...nothing came to mind except this, "JJ, you're in no shape to drive home tonight. You can sleep here if you want, but on the couch."

* * *

When Johnson woke the next morning his skull was throbbing from yesterdays blow to the head. The Jameson didn't help things either. He lay there, completely exposed to the elements with absolutely no memory of the night before. *What have I done?*

Lying next to him in the bed, sound asleep, was JJ. He lifted the sheets and found she wasn't wearing a stitch of clothing either. *She's really something.* He was admiring her curves when she rolled over and opened her large green eyes. *Now what?*

"Mark, I could use some coffee."

And some tooth paste too...

"Let's walk down to the hotel cafe to see if they have anything to eat, or at least get a cup of coffee," she said.

Confused and embarrassed by the situation he said to her, "JJ look, I have no recollection of what we did or didn't do last night or how we ended up here in the sack together. Did we...?"

"I think so... But I'm not remembering all of the details all that clearly either."

"Great. I'd just like to take a hot shower and go home...that is if I still have one."

"Mark, I do know this much, if we did do it, we didn't use any sort of protection."

"What? You're not...ahh...well, aren't you on the pill?"

"No. I had to stop," she said, starting to cry a little. "The increased estrogen level led to irregular cycles. Last night should never have happened...not with you." JJ was trying to choose her words carefully. She wanted to keep him interested in her, at least for a few more months.

Johnson's head was throbbing and his thoughts were racing. He was thinking about the worst-case scenario...and of course his Chao. "Well if it did happen, JJ, we'll have to deal with whatever comes next. For now, we need to stay focused on the case and figure out how to take down Frasier and McDermott?"

"Mark, I'm the Medical Examiner for Humboldt County. I'm not a cop. Trouble is, since becoming involved on this taskforce to smoke out Frasier, I've learned that I can't trust anyone in the Sheriff's department. They're all suspect."

Johnson was having a difficult time focusing. "Maybe we need to bump it up a notch and get the Feds involved. Either the FBI or the DEA."

"DEA?"

"The Drug Enforcement Agency. They may be interested since this case involves a network of pot growers. I think they're the right agency for us to invite in to help."

"Should I contact any of the other task force members to let them know?"

"No. If any of them *are* as rotten as you say, we don't want to tip our hand. I've got a contact in the Sacramento DEA office. I'll call him later."

"I'll get dressed and head down to the café on my own, Mark."

"That's fine. I'll be down in fifteen minutes."

* * *

Johnson's cell phone was buzzing when he stepped out of the shower. "Paula, what's up?"

"How are you feeling today? Are you able to function?"

"My head is sore, Paula. I was able to interview Doctor James last night and learned that Frasier is being investigated."

"Why?'

"Because he's a bad cop."

"How so?"

"He's taken tons of money by providing armed guards to protect the cash that cannabis growers generate. He's been involved with La Ostra since the beginning. McDermott and Burke used him as the heavy for their extracurricular activities."

"Like what, Mark?"

"Apparently they used him to bribe the National Park Service to shut down the oyster farms in the Tomales Bay region. They wanted to eliminate the competition so they could dominate the oyster market on the West Coast."

"That sounds like a Humboldt County issue to me. We have to avoid jumping in. We need to let them solve this on their own or bring in the feds. We have to stay focused on Marin County crimes."

"You're right, Paula."

"That said, we have solid evidence that shows Jacko McDermott was involved in the fires. But we don't know why...we still need a motive."

"Right. So help me figure out what I should be looking for here in Eureka?" Paula heard the hotel room door open and JJ's voice as she bounded in, rather loudly, with a cup of coffee for Johnson.

"Mark," said JJ, "There's a full breakfast buffet down in the café. Let's go down and get something to eat. It ends at nine thirty."

"Who the hell is that, Mark?" asked Chen.

"Doctor James...ahh...JJ for short. She rescued me yesterday."

"What is she doing in your hotel room, Mark?"

John C. LaBella

"Listen, I don't need a lecture from you too. Chao was really torqued last night. It will take a long time for her to forgive me."

"So what got Chao torqued? Mark, did you have relations with that woman? That JJ?" asked Chen using her best Clinton imitation.

"Paula, you've got the wrong impression."

"Well jeez, Mark. Let's see, you've got a strange woman in your hotel room and you obviously spent the night with her. So excuse me. What in the hell impression should I have?"

"OK, Paula, enough. Nothing happened. I got hit over the head yesterday and..."

"Yah, I know. You called yesterday to tell me that, Mark. Did you ever bother to call Chao?"

"Well no. It just sort of got away from me."

"It got away from you? She's your wife. How in the hell did it 'sort of get away' from you?"

"We had dinner near the hotel...JJ and I. We had a couple of drinks and that led to more drinking. After the bar closed we somehow ended up in my hotel room...way too drunk to function."

"So you...?"

"No. We never did. At least we don't remember if we did."

"Mark. Ya gotta keep that thing in its cage."

"Paula, you knew going in, that having a drunk as your backup was a bad idea."

"Knock off the bullshit, Mark. You are one of the best in the business when you manage to keep your drinking problem and your *little Johnson* under control."

There was silence and then Johnson sheepishly said, "Thanks, Paula," followed by silence.

"When are you planning to come home, Mark?"

"Early afternoon today. I was going to spend the morning looking for anything that might help us figure out a motive behind the fires."

"It's almost like they were started at random by some off-the-wall nut-job."

"Paula, we've been in this business long enough to know that crimes like this are rarely a random event. There's a reason, there always is – we just haven't asked the right questions yet."

"It's time for us to have another session at the whiteboard, Mark."

"No. Right now it's time for breakfast."

Chapter 27

Not a word was said as Johnson and JJ walked along the garden path leading to the café. Mark couldn't stop thinking about his conversation with Paula, more importantly he couldn't stop thinking about Chao. *How could I disappoint her again?* He felt awkward walking with JJ. Actually, he wasn't at all comfortable with the entire situation. She was a *Perfect Ten*, but the two had *zero* in common, save basic sexual attraction. He struggled as he searched for something to say. The best he could come up with was, "So, JJ. What's on the buffet?"

"The usual. Instant scrambled eggs – made from a mix – over-cooked sausage patties, cut up fruit, and oatmeal. Oh, I almost forgot, there's one of those waffle makers too."

"Healthy," he said sarcastically, "I can't wait."

As they sat at their table the silence continued to grow. Johnson had powdered eggs with a sprinkle of cheese on them. JJ asked Johnson to pass the jelly for her toast. He did. Then he asked if she would pass the salt and pepper. This went on for twenty minutes until finally she looked at him and said, "Mark. Look, I'm really sorry this got so far out of hand. I'm disappointed in myself for getting you into trouble with your wife. Do you think you'll be able to mend your relationship?"

"JJ. I'm flawed in many different ways. I've been a drunk all my life, but through it all, my wife, my Chao, has always been there for me. I'm praying that she won't give up on me now. If you and I did what we think we might have done last night, it could really change things for us both. It's important to know if we actually did it, or if we didn't."

"Mark, I don't remember what went on last night." Then she took his hand and looked into his eyes, "When I get back to the clinic I'll check myself out and see what, if anything, actually did happen. OK?"

"Listen, I want you to know that I won't ever abandon you if you do become preg..."

JJ cut him off, "Stop it. You don't have to worry about that. I'm a doctor. I can take care of myself, Mark. Don't give it a second thought."

Johnson sat in silence at the table. *Did JJ mean that she was financially capable of raising a child on her own or did she mean she would end the pregnancy?*

* * *

Later that day Paula, Jurek and Johnson were at the whiteboard. "Mark, you seem miles away. What ya' thinking?" asked Chen.

"I just keep drawing blanks on a motive. One more time, from the top."

Chen started, "OK. First of all we've got two women who died here in Tomales."

"Both died as a result of arson," added Jurek.

The squad room door flew open as Jonah Chiang burst into the room. "News flash, guys. Each of our victims tested positive for Oleandrin poisoning. Mark's question about the tea led me to look further. I found it in their tissue and also in their teacups. Put that one on the board, Paula."

"Thanks, Jonah. That's big. We also know that Burke and McDermott had been involved from the get go," said Johnson. "They were the money guys behind La Ostra, LLC."

"And La Ostra LLC recently purchased the three houses that burned in Tomales," added Chen. "I know that Burke's death isn't ours to solve, but it sure looks suspicious due to the similarity. The ME in Humboldt County found the same poison in Burke. What's her name, Mark? The ME."

"Doctor Jillian James. JJ for short."

"Right, Doctor James told you that she found Oleandrin in Burke's tissue and also traces of it in the teacups in his cabin," said Paula.

"So, does that mean that Paddy Burke is linked to our fires too?" asked Jurek.

"That's a good gap question, Jurek. What else, guys? Come on, we need to fill the board," said Johnson. "We know that Detective Frasier has been under investigation for being in bed with La Ostra. There's that other guy too, Milford Neville. He lives in the woods near Eureka."

"Mark, you told me you were hit over the head when you were questioning McDermott. Any idea who clubbed you?" asked Chen.

"I'm not sure. Frasier and I were talking to McDermott when the lights went out. It could have been anyone."

"Could it have been Neville?" asked Chen.

"Let's suppose it was," said Jurek. "For the time being maybe we should assume that Neville was the one who hit Mark. At least until we come up with a different suspect."

"McDermott and Neville were in Tomales the night of the fires, at least the second fire, per the video evidence and eyewitness accounts," said Chen. "But I don't think we have enough to convince the DA to charge them yet. We need a damn motive."

"Mark. You said you were working with Doctor James in Eureka. I tried to call her but couldn't get through," said Jonah. "So I checked to see if there was an alternate number for her on the Medical Board of California's website. Guess what? There's no Doctor James listed."

"She must be on it, Jonah. I think that James is her married name. She may have registered under her maiden name when she finished med school. Or maybe she changed it after her husband died."

"Husband?" asked Chen. "That's probably it. So how did her husband die?"

"She said that he was involved in some sort of a diving accident," said Johnson. "Listen, I know she's a doctor. She's the ME in Humboldt County so that means she has to be a doctor, right, Jonah?"

"Yes. In order to be the ME in a large county one needs to be a doctor and also have four years of training in forensic pathology."

"She's the person Frasier called when Burke was found tits up in his cabin."

"Are you sure she's not a coroner? They don't have to be doctors," said Chen.

"No. She's not a coroner. She told me she was a doctor and when Frasier introduced us, he called her *Doctor James*," Johnson was getting rather defensive about the line of questioning concerning JJ.

"OK. I'm sorry I got us off-track," said Jonah.

"Let's move on. What else do we have for the whiteboard?" asked Chen. "What do we know about the cancer the two victims had?"

"Sure. It could have been caused by the type of radiation in the waters near the Farallon Islands."

"But Jonah, those islands are twenty some miles from Tomales Bay," said Johnson.

"Here's the thing, oysters feed by absorbing whatever's in the water around them. Over time, radioactive material may have accumulated in the oysters. It's possible that the women picked up a lethal dose of rads from oyster shucking."

"English please, Jonah?" asked Chen.

"Sorry. A rad is short for a Radiation Absorbed Dose. It's a measure of the amount of radiation a person has absorbed."

"And don't forget that picture in the lobby of the hotel," added Jurek. "Three of the four shuckers in the picture have been diagnosed with cancer."

"We should measure the radiation levels in our two victims and in the two survivors," said Jonah.

"If you can do that Jonah, the results would tell us for sure if the radiation dumped at the Farallones is linked to the cancers."

"Easy peasy, Mark. I'll have my guys test the victim's tissue in the lab and send a tech to test the other two women with a Geiger counter. We should know later today. Say, Jurek, I have an address for Tilly Martinson. I need one for your Grandmother."

"Let us know as soon as you know, Jonah. So let's pursue a thought line in the event that the radioactive waste at the Farallones *is* the cause," said Chen. "So, what? What's the big deal if it is?"

"Well for starters," said Johnson. "If the victims proved they were exposed to radiation from oyster shucking, the law suits would be huge."

"It would also create mass confusion and panic in the population living anywhere within fifty miles of the islands – and that's the entire San Francisco Bay area," said Jurek.

"Don't forget, those lawsuits would ultimately lead back to the oyster farms."

"Right, Paula," said Johnson. "Who ever owns the Dream Bay Oyster Company, as well as any of the other grow-outs, could be facing financial ruin from litigation. Killing these women would certainly delay or even stop all pending legal action. That's gotta be the best motive we have."

"It sure is," said Jurek. "So, who owns the Dream Bay Oyster Company? I believe the answer to that question could lead us to our killer."

"Why don't you guys take fifteen? I'll walk down to the Marin County Register of Deeds Office and check to see if I can find the answer to that question," said Johnson. As he was walking down the hall to the Register of Deeds office, his phone buzzed. It was JJ.

"Hi Mark. Remember me?"

"Who could forget you, JJ? What do you want?"

"How about dinner tonight? I'm driving down to the city. I'll be there by five thirty."

"Are you traveling down here for business or pleasure, JJ?"

"Well, actually I was hoping for a little of each, Mark. I'd like to discuss the case with you. Then afterward maybe there'll be time for pleasure?"

"Listen, JJ. You're a wonderful woman and I enjoy working with you. However, I don't think we can continue the personal relationship we started."

"Fine," she said, "But we do have something we need to discuss, Pops."

Chapter 28

"What'cha looking for?" asked Megan Plennard. Johnson was wading through three-inch thick books of deed transfers but thinking about the call from JJ. He hadn't noticed Meg walk in. She was Assistant to the Marin County Register of Deeds.

"Hi, Meg," said Johnson, a bit startled. "I'm looking for transactions relating to the Dream Bay Oyster Company."

"Well, Honey, you're in the wrong book. This room has sales and exchanges for residential real estate. Business transactions are in a different book in a totally separate room."

"Really? I didn't know that."

"Come on, I'll take you there." He followed Meg to a small room next to the main file room. It was dimly lit and smelled of musty old paper. There was a small table with an old oak desk chair – the kind that swivels. "Here you go, Mark. Can I help you find what ever it is you're looking for?"

"No thanks, Meg. I'll just browse through the book on my own if you don't mind."

"No problem. I'll be at my desk in case you need something." Johnson proceeded to work his way through the book. Organized by sale date, each book was rather heavy and contained about five years of transactions. Johnson figured the sale of Dream Bay had to be recent, certainly within the past five to ten years. Starting with the most recent book, he paged through it slowly, his eyes scanning for the words, *Dream Bay*. Then he found it. Two years ago the Dream Bay Oyster Company was sold to La Ostra, LLC. *This is a huge break...*

Johnson went back to the squad room and announced, "Anyone want to take a guess on who the current owner of Dream Bay is?"

"No kidding? Its La Ostra, isn't it?" asked Chen.

"On the nose, Paula. La Ostra, LLC bought the Dream Bay Oyster Company two years ago and had it shuttered within six months."

"Eureka," yelled Jonah, another failed attempt at humor. "Get it?" he asked, "Come on, the LLC is based in Eureka..." The others just looked at him.

"That was around the time the National Parks Service had discontinued the leases on oyster grow-outs on Tomales Bay. Dream Bay was an exception, they were not on leased land," said Johnson.

"So why did La Ostra buy it?" asked Jurek.

"Maybe they wanted the equipment," said Chen.

"Or rights to the name," added Jonah.

"Dream Bay was the last competitor on Tomales Bay. The point is they own it and could be held libel for past issues, even if the sellers weren't aware of them," said Johnson. "Like the radiation exposure."

"Did you notice if there was an indemnification clause in the contract?" asked Jurek.

"What's that?" asked Chen.

"An indemnity agreement from the seller would mean that any unknown or unforeseen liabilities that arise after the sale would remain the responsibility of the seller," said Chiang.

"I didn't notice anything like that in the transfer documents," replied Johnson. "The sale contract isn't in the Register of Deeds records – just the documents for the transfer of the deed."

"I'm going out on a limb," said Paula, "and suggest that there was no indemnification clause in the purchase agreement. The result of which means La Ostra could be facing huge lawsuits due to the cancer...a cancer caused by radiation absorbed by Dream Bay employees who worked in the shucking room. I believe the motive behind the fires was to prevent the victims from suing La Ostra, LLC. Thoughts anyone?"

"Makes sense," said Johnson. "Does anyone not agree with the motive Paula so eloquently stated?" All were in agreement. "Good, let's issue warrants for the arrest of McDermott and Neville. What about Detective Frasier?"

"Sticky, Mark. We should contact the Humboldt County Executive to let him know," said Chen.

"I've also tipped off the DEA," said Johnson.

"Great job everyone," said Chiang. "Once the arrests are made and we get a confession, we need to celebrate. This has been a very complicated case."

"As you said, Jonah, we need a confession before considering this case closed. I know it's early, but I'm heading out. I've got a few things to deal with, starting with my wife, Chao."

On his way home, Johnson called Chao's cell. No answer. *She's really upset with me, and I can't blame her.* Johnson dreaded the thought that his marriage to Chao may soon be over. He began to think about how he would explain to his kids that their father was a drunk who had been unfaithful to their mom. A few seconds later his phone buzzed; "Hi, Babe," he said, thinking it was Chao. "I'm on my way home. We need to talk."

"Absolutely," said the voice on the other end, "We do need to talk..."

"JJ. What do you want?"

"Like you said, we need to talk. Let's discuss our future over dinner tonight. Come on. I'll buy."

Johnson was furious and yet, intrigued. Upset by the fact that this woman had created an irreparable chasm between he and his wife, at the same time, he was curious to learn why she had called him "Pops." He had to talk to her. He tried to think of a place to meet that was private and quiet enough to talk, and yet at the same time, a top shelf place to assure she would not go ballistic. Finally he came up with a location, "Let's meet at Billy's House of Prime Rib at six-thirty. It's on Van Ness."

"Fine, Mark. I'll meet you in the lounge."

Johnson arrived at six. The lounge at Billy's was filling fast but he found a small, secluded table in the back of the room. "Just a club soda, please, with a wedge of lime," he told the waiter. "Someone will be joining me so leave the tab open."

"Right away sir."

Johnson's thoughts meandered as he waited for JJ. *Will I be able to fix things with Chao? Is JJ pregnant? Who set the fires?*

However, the topic he couldn't get out of his mind was the one initiated by Jonah. Was JJ really a doctor? He organized his observations. Initially he was sure that she was a doctor. After all Frasier called her to Burke's cabin and introduced her as

"Doctor James." She wore a white coat, scrubs and had a stethoscope. However, these things alone could not validate whether she was a doctor or not. After all, anyone can buy a white coat and scrubs. And why on earth did she carry a stethoscope to a death investigation?

The next time they met at Burke's cabin, JJ was giving him mouth-to-mouth. He was glad she did but later, when she walked him into the ER, nobody addressed her as "Doctor James," no one even recognized her. She was treated as if she was a total stranger. It's logical to assume that in a small town the size of Eureka, medical professionals would know each other. Then he realized that he had never actually seen her in a clinical setting.

"JJ. Over here," Johnson called out when she walked into the lounge. She was gorgeous. Her auburn hair danced atop her shoulders accenting her neck and the low cut red dress she wore. Johnson was flummoxed.

"Hi Mark," she said as she neared the table. "My eyes need a minute to adjust. Did you order me a drink yet? I could sure use one."

"Waiter. A Rusty Nail for the lady."

"Right away, Sir."

Johnson turned to JJ and just came out with it, "Where did you go to medical school?"

"UCSF, Mark. Right here in San Francisco. Why do you ask?"

"I'm just curious." Johnson was silent. Then he continued, "I'm having a difficult time proving in my mind that you're a real doctor, JJ."

"What do you mean, Mark?"

"For starters, you don't show up on the State's website of registered physicians and the only other person who addressed you as *Doctor* was Frasier, and I don't trust him."

"Whoever told you that I wasn't on the Medical Board's website probably didn't search for me under my maiden name. It's Loomis." Johnson paused for a moment when he heard her maiden name. *Loomis? I wonder if she's related to Grace or Jimmy Loomis?*

"I never went through the process of legally changing my name after getting married. I used my husband's name on everything and nobody, at least until now, ever questioned it."

"What was your husband's name?"

"Malcolm James."

"So, you never legally changed it after you got married? You just used your husband's name on checking accounts, credit cards, etc. And you never changed your professional licensure on the State's Website? That doesn't make sense, JJ. Would you mind showing me your credentials?"

"No, Mark. I don't mind showing you. I don't understand why you're questioning my credibility."

"I'm not questioning anything. I just don't have any proof that you are what you say you are."

"Mark, I don't carry my State Board ID on me. It's in the top drawer in my office desk."

"Call someone in Eureka and ask them to take a picture of it and send it to you. I really need to see it." Johnson wasn't letting up and JJ knew it.

"Mark, you're acting crazy. Didn't I perform the autopsy? Didn't I save your life?"

"Yes, you did. But none of that proves you are a real medical doctor."

JJ knew she was losing the battle and decided to change the narrative, "Mark," she said in a soft, gentle voice, "I want you. I've wanted you from the first moment I saw you. I want you so bad I can feel it in my soul." She took his hand and put it up to her cheek, rubbing her face with the back of his hand. She looked into his eyes, moved a little closer and kissed him. "Mark," she said in very low, sexy voice, "Let's get out of here. I've booked a room down on Lombard Street. Come on, Mark. Come with me now, or stay here in your world forever." JJ got up and left. Johnson was confused. *Should I follow her or not?* He paid the bill and walked out.

Chapter 29

"JJ. Wait up," Johnson called as he ran down the street after her. "Wait. I need to talk to you." JJ kept walking down Van Ness Street.

After one more block, she turned to him and abruptly asked, "Why? What do you want Mark?"

"I need to know..." he said panting and out of breath. "I need to know why you called me Pops?"

"Maybe because you're the father of this kid inside me," she said pointing to her belly. "By the way, in case you haven't figured it out yet, yes, we did do it in that hotel room in Eureka. It was great. Too bad you were too drunk to remember it."

"Come on, JJ. That was three days ago and you already know you're pregnant? What's going on? What do you want from me?"

"I want you to take responsibility for this kid and be a father to him, Mark. That's what I want."

"Listen, JJ. We both know I'm not the father of your kid. I'm ready to go do a DNA test right now.

In fact, I'm willing to bet that there's no trace of me in you at all. I don't think we did a damn thing in that hotel room. You're trying to extort me, JJ and that's against the law."

JJ began to cry. "I don't know what to do, Mark. I was desperate these past few weeks. I screwed up big time as you can see. I was hoping that you would be my white knight."

"JJ, you need help – more help than I can give you. Are you able to go to your parents?"

"Fat chance of that happening."

"You told me your maiden name was Loomis. Do you even know who or where your parents are? Do they live in California anymore?"

"No idea. My mother got knocked up by my father one night and nine months later I was put up for adoption."

"How did you pick Loomis as your last name?"

"After I graduated from Medical School I was able to get access to adoption records across the state. So I correlated the dates of my own adoption and figured out that my mother was just sixteen years old when she gave birth to me."

"And your father? Was there a father's name on the birth record or a location or something?"

"Of course there was, that's why I decided to go by Loomis. That guy knocked up my mother when the two of them were teenagers. They were both dirt poor – neither had a pot to piss in."

"I'm sorry to hear that, JJ. I'd be happy to help you but I've got a family of my own to take care of. I've got a wife, a beautiful woman who has devoted her entire life to me and three..."

"Mark, you'll see," she said interrupting him, "I'll be just as devoted to you as she's been."

"JJ, you'll never be my wife. You need to realize that." As he said that, she took a scalpel from her purse and put it to her neck. "What are you doing?"

"You don't think I'm a real doctor? I learned this trick in Med School. If I cut right here," she said pointing to her jugular vein, "I'll bleed out before you can dial nine-one-one."

"For God's sake, JJ. Don't do that. Think of the baby you have living in you. Think of the life you've got in front of you. Think of me for a minute. How will I explain this to the people you leave behind?"

"Who's that? The guy who knocked me up?" My parents...Who? Nobody gives a shit about me."

"JJ, I promise that I'll put you in touch with people who'll help you. Just for the record, can you tell me who the father of your baby is?"

"For the record? What record?" After a pause she said, "What the hell, its Frasier's. I've been his office whore for a few years and got careless."

"For Christ's sake, JJ. Does he know? What about the investigation on him?"

"No. I haven't told him that he's gonna be a daddy caus' I'm not sure if I'm keeping it," she paused, "but I hate the idea of killing it just because I screwed up. Oh, and I cooked up that story about an investigation on him just to draw you closer to me. He's a pretty solid guy and sure was pissed when I hit you with that ball bat."

"You hit me? Why?"

"I da know. I guess I didn't want you to put the chains on McDermott and haul him away."

"Why in the hell were you there in the first place? Did Frasier bring you?"

"No. I was there visiting my father."

"Wait. Are you saying McDermott's your father?

"Sort of. That old pussy took me in when I was a kid. He adopted me and raised me until I went off to medical school. I hid in the back room when you and Frasier got there. I knew why you were there. I just couldn't sit there and let you arrest him."

"So, I suppose Jacko will miss you, right?"

"Yah, sure, I suppose he will."

Desperate to get the knife from her and resolve the situation peacefully he said, "I think I know who your real father is, JJ. Was his name James Loomis?"

"Yeah. How did you know that?" she asked.

"I ran into him a few days ago." JJ's eyes, smudged from tears, had a desperate sort of *killer* look in them – a look that scared Johnson. *Shit, she's gonna do it.* "JJ," he said in his authoritative police voice, "Drop the knife right now." After a pause, JJ dropped the scalpel. She stood there sobbing as Johnson put his arms around her. He held her tight telling her, "I'll arrange for you to meet your father soon." Johnson then transported JJ to the Langley Porter Mental Health Clinic on Parnassus Avenue. He admitted her for a psych evaluation.

Still thinking about Chao, and not knowing how she'd react to him, he decided to go home in hopes of seeing her. Johnson had been gone for almost seventy-two hours. Still, he prayed that Chao would be there and maybe even speak to him.

Chapter 30

The late afternoon shadows had sucked the last bit of sunlight out of Johnson's tea garden. It was sweater weather and Chao was wrapped in her bulky cable knit. A blanket on her lap kept her warm as she sat alone in the garden. The bench she was on held memories for her, mostly the many long conversations she had with Mark. Her hand moved along the oak slats, smooth from years of use. She could feel Mark's presence.

Chao tried not to think about him. *I need to get the house ready for Christmas. Will the girls stay here or will they stay with friends as they had for Thanksgiving?* She began weeping heavily as she sat bundled up in her blanket. Chao tried to imagine what Christmas without Mark would be like. She wasn't looking forward to it.

Johnson accepted that Chao had thrown him out of the house but he had to stop for a few things. *There's a light on. Is Chao at home?* It was still his house

275

but to be polite, he rang the bell. No answer. However, to his surprise his key still worked. He looked for her in the living room first, then in the kitchen and finally in the bedrooms – no sign of her. *The tea garden...?*

"Who's there?" Chao asked, as she heard the back door open. Not knowing it was Johnson she raised her voice and said, "My husband's a cop."

"No, lady. Your husband's an idiot."

"Mark? Is that you? I'm over here on my seat."

"Do you want some company?"

"No. What I want is a husband I can trust. A husband who is dedicated to me...to us."

"Chao, I'm so sorry. I swear nothing happened between JJ and me."

"Bullshit, Buster. You were in a hotel room with another woman. That *did* happen. Right? Whether you were drunk or sober, whether you screwed her or not isn't important. Well, it's important but that's a matter of physiology and basic animal instinct. The fact is you betrayed me. You betrayed the trust I had in you. That's what really hurts."

"I got drunk and she helped me into the room."

"You got drunk...so that makes it ok? Tell me, Mark, did she help you out of your pants too? Did you help her out of hers? Did you force her to stay with you all night?"

"What are you talking about, Chao?"

"I was there, Asshole."

"What do you mean, you were there?"

"You know, like I got in my car and drove for five hours. That's what I mean by *I was there*."

"Chao, why? Did Paula call you?"

"No. Paula didn't call. The ER in Eureka did. I am, or used to be, an ICE contact on your phone."

"ICE? Oh, right, In Case of Emergency?"

"Yes, Mark. So they called me to say you had a possible skull fracture. What was I supposed to do? Sit here at home and assume your hot little redhead would take care of you?"

"Chao, I had no idea."

"You had no idea? What, that I might catch you taking a woman into your room? Your loyalty to me is all you should need to keep your dick in your pants, not the fear of getting caught."

"I came to apologize to you, Chao. I wanted to tell you that I'm ready to change but it seems that you're not ready to talk about that yet."

"Oh, believe me, I'm ready too. I've put up with your habits, your drinking and your skirt chasing for over twenty years. Am I ready for a change? You can bet your ass I am, buster."

"Me too, Chao. I want to be the man you fell in love with. I want to grow old with you and..."

"Get the hell out of the house right now." Chao cut him off before he finished his thought. "I want you gone. Go live with your redheaded slut-friend, Mark. I don't want you here anymore."

"She's psychotic, Chao. She tried to slit her own throat with a scalpel. I dropped her off at Langley Porter before coming here."

"Too bad for her. That woman is way too frail to put up with your bullshit, Mark. Have a good life. Now get the hell out of my house."

A despondent Johnson grabbed a few shirts, an extra pair of jeans, some underwear and a pair of shoes. He stuffed all of it into two Safeway grocery bags. Chao watched him walk out. As the door closed behind him, hot tears ran down her face.

* * *

Johnson's cell phone vibrated with a call, "Hey, Mark, it's Paula. Where are you?"

"I'm out driving around. I was thinking about the case. My head hurts like hell and oh yes, Chao kicked me out for good."

"Sorry to hear that, Mark. You can stay with me tonight if you need a place to crash."

"Thanks, Paula. I'll get a hotel room for tonight, I really want to be alone right now."

"Sure, Mark. I understand. Say, listen, I just got word that Jimmy Loomis is dead."

"Whoa. What happened to Jimmy?"

"Angus drove down here to pick him up. The two of 'em apparently drove back to that mule farm that the McGee family runs."

"Car accident?"

"No, Jimmy got kicked by one of the mules."

"No way. Kicked in the head?"

"Apparently they were trying to bust one of 'em and the damned mule kicked Jimmy right square in the nads. He was kicked so hard that his jewels were driven pretty far up into his chest cavity."

"Oh my God. Jeez. That must of hurt."

"Ya' think?"

Chapter 31

Jurek, Paula and Johnson were seated around the squad room table. "What's up, Mark?" asked Jurek. "You look like you just lost your best friend."

"I have..." he started, but decided not to share anything about he and Chao. "Paula, do we have enough to issue an arrest warrant for McDermott?"

"I believe we do. We have an eye witness that puts him and his accomplice, Milton Neville, in Tomales on the night of the most recent fire."

"I think his name is Milford, not Milton," Jurek said, correcting Paula.

"What's the damn difference?" grumbled Paula, as she walked over to the coffee pot.

"We have to be sure to use the correct name on the warrant," said Mark.

"And what about Detective Frasier? How deep is he involved?" asked Paula? "I mean, as long as we're in Humboldt County to nab McDermott, do we want to grab Frasier too?"

"I da know," said Johnson starting to waffle a bit. "According to JJ he's a straight-shooter."

"Wait a minute," said Jurek, "Not more than twenty hours ago you told us that JJ said he was under investigation for his dealings with La Ostra. Now you're telling us that he's clean?"

"JJ's initial story was flawed."

"What the hell, Mark? What do you mean her story was flawed? Spill it..." Paula was furious with Johnson and didn't hide it. He had misled them by not updating JJ's story the moment it changed.

"Paula, please. I don't want to get into this right now. We can get into the details later. For now just understand that Frasier's not a dirty cop."

"Jurek, could you check to see if Dr. Chiang is in his lab? I'd like him to weigh in on something." She really wanted was to talk to Johnson in private.

"Sure thing, Paula," said Jurek.

After Jurek left, Paula stood toe to toe with Johnson, "Give me the whole story – now."

"OK. You knew about JJ and I ending up in my hotel room. Right?"

"Yes, but you told me nothing happened."

"Right, but she made me believe that we had a physical relationship. In fact, she tried to get me to believe that I had knocked her up."

"Oh no. Did you?"

"Did I what?"

"Did you knock her up?"

"Paula, no. I didn't get her pregnant. That deed was done well before I met her. She latched onto me to be her 'sugar-daddy' and help raise her kid."

"So then, what's the big deal, Mark?"

"The big deal is that Chao got a call from the ER in Eureka telling her that I was being admitted for a possible skull fracture. She drove up to Eureka and said that she found us in my room. That's why she kicked me out. I was too damn drunk to realize she was even there."

"When I need a good detective, maybe I should hire her. How in the hell was she able to find you?"

"I guess she started at the ER. When she learned I was released, she checked hotels near the hospital until she found my car. She told the desk clerk that she was my wife and they gave her a room key."

"So she found you with JJ? Holy shit."

"I know. I told her that I was drunk and nothing happened. She said it didn't matter. She said I had violated her trust and booted me out of the house."

"I'd have to agree with her, Mark. Now what?"

"There's more."

"Oh boy, I can't wait."

"JJ came to town to talk and we met for dinner. I explained that I was happily married and was in no way interested in her. Then I guess I pressed a little too hard about whether she was a real doctor or not. I'm afraid that sent her over the edge."

"So did she prove she was a doctor?"

"Well no. Not conclusively. I pushed her to the point where she became an emotional wreck. She begged me to come with her to her hotel room. When I refused, she abruptly left the restaurant. I followed her down Van Ness. When I caught up to her she told me that she was pregnant and wanted me to help her raise the kid."

"Shit, Mark. Did you knock her up or not? You're not making any sense."

"No, I never touched her. She told me she's pregnant and definitely has a baby bump, but it ain't mine. Then she pulled out a scalpel, right there on the street, and threatened to slit her throat with it. She's really whacked up, Paula."

"Boy oh boy, I guess so."

"I talked her down and then admitted her to the psych ward at Langley Porter," Johnson started to tear up a little. "When I went home to explain things to Chao I found her in the tea garden. It was ugly, Paula. She said she was done with me and threw me out. I don't know what to do..."

"Mark, we're close to making the final arrests in the arson case. Once it's over, you need to check into rehab and get sober. There's no guarantee you'll get her back if you do that. However, I *can* guarantee there's no way in hell you'll get her back if you don't. You have to get sober."

"You're right, Paula. You're right..."

"So, Mark. If you weren't the one who got JJ pregnant, who did?"

"She told me it was Frasier's. She told me that he had been using his position of authority to make her his office bitch. He took liberties with her and she went along to get along. Eventually she slipped up and got herself into trouble."

"That son-of-a-bitch. I thought you said he was clean, Mark."

"He's clean from a corruption perspective but a filthy pig when it comes to how he treated JJ."

"I'd like to fry that guy but we need him to get to McDermott and Neville. I'll have to wait."

"I think you're right. I'll call off the DEA."

"Sure. We won't need them," said Chen. "Wait, why in the hell did you contact them, Mark?"

"Because I was told that Frasier was in bed with La Ostra's weed money. I thought they would be interested because it involves drugs. I'll call and ask them to stand down."

"Is there anything else I need to know before we round up the bad guys?"

"No. That's it. I need this case to be over so I can complete my obligation to Forrest."

"No, Mark. You need this case to be over so you can get your life back. Let's get Jurek and drive up to Eureka to nab the bad guys."

Chapter 32

Johnson was driving Paula and Jurek to Eureka. "I'm gonna call Frasier," said Chen. "May I speak to Detective Frasier?" After a brief wait, Frasier picked up. "Hello, Detective. Paula Chen here. I'm on my way to Eureka with a few deputies. We have warrants for the arrest of Jacko McDermott and Milford Neville. Of course, we'd welcome your help and cooperation with this."

"Sure. We'll help. By the way, how is Detective Johnson? He took quite a blow to the head."

"Yes, he's lucky to have such a hard head."

"Funny. But he could've died without the help he got from Doctor James. She was able to revive him and get him to the ER just in time."

"Tell me Frasier, how is it she was on hand at McDermott's cabin to save him?" Chen was testing to see if he would tell the truth or get caught in a lie.

"Well, I don't rightly know," he said. "Maybe she was seeing patients in the commune?"

"I'd like to speak to her when we get there."

"Sure. I'll set that up, Detective Chen."

"Thank you." *What a pig.* Paula had a hard time accepting the fact that Frasier had used the power of his position to take advantage of a woman. *I'm going to nail that bastard for what he did to Doctor James.*

"I'll go ahead and ask the Humboldt County DA to issue warrants for the arrest of Mister Neville and Mister McDermott," said Frasier.

"No need, Detective. I told you that we have warrants, they were issued from the Marin County bench because the crimes they're being arrested for occurred in Marin."

"Not so fast, Detective Chen. We still have the case of Paddy Burke's murder to account for. It just so happens that Jacko McDermott is at the top of our suspect list for that one."

"Consider this. The first murder took place in Marin County and we have enough evidence to arraign him. We'll add Burke's murder to the list of charges but first we'll need the Humboldt County DA's rationale for charging him; things such as motive, method, opportunity, etc. Do you think you can convince a jury that he did it?"

"We sure do. I'll talk to the DA shortly and have an answer for you by the time you arrive."

"That's fine. In the mean time I'll contact Jack Gordon to get his take on how to proceed."

"Now wait a minute. There's no need to get the AG involved...is there?" Jack Gordon has been the Attorney General for the State of California since the mid-nineties. He knew how to get convictions. Chen was sure he would want the suspects tried in Marin County Superior Court.

"Listen," said Chen. "I've got enough evidence to convict them on Arson and Murder-One. I don't think you've got your case together yet...do you?"

"Oh? I think we do. I'll contact Doctor James and get her statement about the poisoning. She's an eyewitness to the attack on Detective Johnson too."

"We can go over the doctor's statement when I get there." Paula knew that Frasier was completely disorganized and didn't have a chance of getting any statement from Doctor James right now. He didn't know that she was in a psych ward in San Francisco.

"Maybe we should have two trials," suggested Detective Frasier.

What an idiot. "I'll run that idea by Gordon when I speak to him," Paula said to appease him. *There's no way in hell that will happen.* Paula knew there would be one trial with multiple charges.

"OK. I'll send my guys out to McDermott's place and round em' up. I'm not sure where Neville is but we'll find him too. Don't worry, we'll find them for you, Detective Chen."

"Thanks, Detective Frasier. We should be there in another hour or so." Paula had a feeling that the arrest of McDermott would not go smoothly.

"What's new with Frasier?" asked Johnson.

"Not much. He wants them arraigned up there."

"That's crazy. The crimes were committed in Marin County and that's where..."

Chen cut him off. "That's right. But if Jacko McDermott is bound over for Burke's murder before we pick him up, we're screwed."

"Yah, but he's got a flimsy case."

"And his star witness, JJ, is in the psych ward – that'll devalue her testimony," added Jurek.

"Right, guys. I'm on the same wavelength as you are on this. I'm going to call Jack Gordon just to be sure he's in agreement with our approach."

"Good idea, Paula. Let us know how that goes."

"I'll call him right now. Feel free to listen in." Chen knew Gordon from his days as City Attorney in San Francisco. "Jack Gordon, please," she said to the young man answering the phones.

"I'm sorry, but Mister Gordon is not available at this time," said the young man. "I'd be happy to take a message. May I ask who is calling?"

"Sure, tell him that Paula Chen would appreciate a call back."

"Can I have your number, Ma'am?"

"He's got it. We worked together for years," said Paula, hoping it would facilitate a callback. Gordon called a few minutes later. Paula explained her plan to him and, as expected, Gordon backed her.

* * *

It was early afternoon and a light rain was falling. The coastal fog was rolling in when Paula and her team arrived at Frasier's office. Two Marin County deputies followed in a second car that would be used to bring the prisoners back. "We're here to see Detective Frasier," Chen told the receptionist. Frasier must have heard her and came out of his office as soon as she asked for him.

"Detective Chen, it's good to see you. How are you doing?"

"One look at my bruises and bandages should help answer that question, you dumb asshole."

"Paula, jeez. Let's lighten up until after we get what we came for," said Johnson under his breath. "No need to piss him off – he's got what we want."

"That's right, Miss Chen. I've got what you want and I control if, and when, you get it," said Frasier.

"You're right, I'm sorry. But that doesn't change the fact that you're an asshole. I've got half a mind to come after you for raping Doctor James."

"What the hell are you talking about?" asked Frasier. "I never forced myself on Miss James."

"Then explain to me how she got pregnant?" asked Johnson. "She says you're the baby-daddy."

"Let me repeat," said Frasier. "What the hell are you talking about? She seemed fine with our 'adult' relationship when she needed a place to stay...for six goddamned months."

"So, you're saying she moved in with you?" asked Johnson. "That's not the way she played it."

"Well go ahead and ask anyone you want. Hey, Bobbie-Jean," Frasier called out to the receptionist. "How long have Doctor James and I been dating?"

"Don't bother answering, Bobbie," said Chen, "Let's focus on the prisoners. Where are they?"

"I sent two men out to McDermott's cabin to arrest them. I just spoke to them and unfortunately, he's holed up and won't come out."

"Let's go. I'll bust that old fart and his little friend Myron myself," said an irate Paula.

"It's Milford, Paula. Not Myron." said Johnson.

"Whatever. Let's get our guys and go get him."

"Do you think you can find his cabin this time or do you want to follow me?"

"We'll follow you," said Paula. "I can't afford any more time in the hospital. Let's move..."

Chapter 33

Chen and her team were following close behind Frasier as he headed south on the 101 to Ferndale. He took the exit that leads to McDermott's cabin. Upon arrival, Frasier's men were dug in outside the cabin. One of them had a shoulder wound. "What's the status here, Bill?" he asked the senior officer.

"That S.O.B. is armed to the teeth, Lieutenant. He cut through us like a buzz saw. He took us by surprise. Frank took one in the shoulder."

"I saw him when we pulled up. How bad is it?" asked Frasier. "Does he need a doctor?"

"It looks like a flesh wound to me. He's lost some blood but he'll be fine. The Paramedics are on their way, I called it in a little while ago."

"What's he got inside with him?"

"It sounded like a semi-automatic assault rifle."

"Dammit, this ends now," said Frasier. "Hey, Jacko. Jacko McDermott. Put your weapons down and get your ass out here right now."

"Put your vests on and grab your weapons," Chen told her guys. "Be prepared for a firefight, we may have to go in after him."

Frasier was miffed. He had always considered McDermott to be a friend. He called him out again. "Last chance to walk away from this, Jacko. Get out here now." Slowly, the cabin door opened and there stood Jacko McDermott. He was wearing coveralls with no shirt under it. His arms were raised over his head but his Squad Automatic Weapon, a SAW 249, was slung over his shoulder and hung about waist-high on a three-inch wide canvas strap. He had nothing on his feet except a pair of comfy looking suede slippers – the kind that one may find at a Janet Reno tag sale.

The two deputies from Marin took up a position covering the back of the cabin. A window was the only exit to the rear. Paula, Johnson and Jurek had taken cover in front of the cabin behind a cord of stacked wood. Two of Frasier's men were out front too. One had taken cover behind a broken down jeep and other behind a tree.

"What the hell do you want with me, Frasier?" asked McDermott.

"You're under arrest for the murders of Grace Loomis and Emily Donegrass in Marin County," barked Frasier. "Now lay down that weapon and get your ass off the porch and get away from the cabin. Don't make us come in after you."

Suddenly, shots were heard coming from the back of the cabin. Milford Neville, armed with a small handgun, had tried to escape through the rear window. The deputies ordered him to stop. Instead, he turned and raised his gun. Bad move on his part.

McDermott took advantage of the diversion caused by the gunfire and grabbed his SAW 249. He let out a bloodcurdling yell, a war cry of sorts. He sounded like a banshee in heat. The SAW 249 is a machine gun, capable of firing over seven hundred rounds per minute. Without warning, he raised it and began shooting everything in sight.

Dirt, debris and glass fragments were flying everywhere. Car windows exploded from the rapid rain of bullets, tires were flattened, and then Frasier went down. The staccato of machine gun fire was deafening. Then, without as much as a second thought, Chen jumped up. As she fired her weapon, she was screamed, "You're going down now, Jacko."

"Holly shit, Paula, get down. Take cover," yelled Johnson. The shooting was over as fast as it had started. McDermott lay dead in the entryway of his cabin. Paula managed to put two slugs in his chest, one in his throat and two in his forehead before she went down herself. "Paula," screamed Johnson. "Paula, are you ok?" She did not answer, as she lay motionless in the dirt. Johnson ran to her side and dropped to both knees. He held her head in his lap, sobbing and pleading with her, "Paula, talk to me," he said, hoping she would respond. He knew that she was in bad shape. Blood was oozing out from behind her vest. For a brief moment, Johnson was transported back to the night that his partner, Tommy Bartlett, was shot. Tommy died in his arms. Now, an eerily similar scenario was playing out with Paula. Johnson was afraid that he knew how this would end...

Chapter 34

"Mark. Come in and have a seat," said Forrest. "Tell me. What in the hell happened up in Eureka?"

"Things got crazy really fast. He had a SAW machine gun and used it to literally mow us down. I've never experienced anything like it."

"Slow down a bit. Who had a SAW?"

"Jacko McDermott. The guy we had suspected was behind the fires. We went up to arrest him."

"Just one guy?"

"Yah. Well, expect for his accomplice, Milford Neville. Our guys put Neville down when he tried to escape through a rear window."

"Was he armed?"

"The dumbass was carrying a snub-nosed thirty-eight special. When he raised it, they cut him down. It was a justified shoot, Denny."

"Tell me a little about that SAW."

"The technical name for it is a Squad Automatic Weapon. That gun is capable of spitting out seven hundred rounds per minute."

"Sounds like that was exactly what it was doing. He didn't need a helper."

"No shit, Denny. And he had it wide open."

"So what happened to Paula?"

"She rushed the bastard to draw fire away from the rest of us. Her piece was drawn and even though she got shot herself, she was able to put four into the guy. She saved us, Denny, but she may have paid the ultimate price."

"Amazing bravery, Mark. Will she make it?"

"Who the hell knows, Denny?"

"Is she still in Eureka?"

"She needed specialists that were not available in Eureka. When she was stable enough for medevac, she was put on a chopper and flown to Parnassus, down in the city. She's in an induced coma due to the severe head trauma and swelling. When I last saw her, the doctors wouldn't speculate on her chances. All they would say was that they were doing everything they could. We're all praying that she survives this, Denny."

"Mark, try to remain positive. I can remember, and not too long ago either, seeing one of my finest detectives as he struggled to survive a shooting. He was in really bad shape too. But dammit, Mark, you pulled through. I'm sure she will too."

"I hope you're right, Denny."

"The report I read said that two died during the arrest. Anymore info on that?"

"As I explained earlier, our guys took down Milford Neville. He was shot as he tried to escape. We have eyewitness accounts placing him along with McDermott at the scene of the fire. And as you know, Paula took down McDermott. That's it."

"How many were wounded?"

"Let's see, Detective Frasier took one in the ass, a bullet I mean. He'll live. One of his guys took a slug in the shoulder. He'll be fine too. Oh, and Paula...how could I forget her."

"So, including the suspects, there are two dead and three wounded. It sounds to me like it would have been a helluva' lot worse if Chen hadn't acted in the way she did."

"I'd agree with that, Denny."

"How are you doing, Mark?"

"Physically I'm fine, Denny. But my life is really messed up and out of control. I need to go home."

Denny went over to Mark, gave him a hug and whispered, "You're dismissed, Mark." As Johnson turned to leave, Forrest gave him a respectful salute and said, "Thank you for your stellar service and for everything you've done for this department."

"I appreciate that, Sir," Johnson went to his office to clean out his desk.

Hot! In Tomales

As he walked to his car carrying a box full of thirty years of stuff, Jonah Chiang caught up with him. "Mark, I heard about the shooting. How's Paula? Anything I can do?"

"Thanks, Jonah. Losing a partner is hard. But Paula was so much more than a partner. She was a lifelong friend. I can't afford to lose her too."

"I know, Mark. I know." Acting like he was hiding something, he said, "I spoke to her attending at Parnassus. It's too early to know her chances."

"I'm heading down to the city to be there for her. I'm just not sure where to go from there or what to do next. I'm sure you've heard that Chao booted me out."

"I heard. You need to go to her, Mark. You two need to get things figured out."

"The girls are pretty much out and on their own now, which leaves Cory as the only person left at home who'll talk to me."

"You're not listening, Mark. You have to find Chao and talk to *her*. Now. Go talk to her, Mark. Tell her how you're feeling and what's going on in your life. That woman idolizes you. You two need each other."

"Right. Thanks for your support, Jonah. I'm going to drive home and see if Cory wants to get a burger or something."

Jonah could see that Johnson was overwhelmed with what was going on in his life. Exhausted and in a daze, Johnson was off in a different place and disconnected from the discussion they were having. *Classic PTSD.* "Call me later, Mark. Maybe we could meet for dinner or something."

"Sure, Jonah. I'll let you know how it goes."

* * *

The sun had set an hour before Johnson pulled up in front of his house. *I'd like to see this place in broad daylight for once.* The house appeared vacant. The porch light, that Chao had asked Johnson to change a few weeks ago, was still out. *I gotta' get that fixed.* Then he noticed a light coming from the back of the house, from the kitchen. Hopeful that Chao would be there, Johnson knocked on the front door.

"Dad." Cory exclaimed when he answered the door. "I was really worried. Are you ok?"

Johnson reached out to give his son a hug. "I'm ok, Cory. But our friend, Paula Chen..."

"I know," Cory said, as he saw the tears welling up in his Dad's eyes. "I'm so sorry. Mom told me all Miss Chen. She told me how the three of you were close in high school and how she had introduced you to Mom."

"And that was the best day of my life," said a voice in the shadows. It was Chao. "Mark...I miss you."

"I miss you too. Can we sit and talk about stuff? I want you to know what I've been dealing with the past few days."

Chao came over to Johnson and put her arms around him. "Cory don't you have homework?"

"Sure, Mom," he said with a grin. "See you guys later."

"Mark, I told you I was there in Eureka. I know what happened. Believe me, that woman didn't want *you* at all. All she wanted was your wallet."

"But Chao, I feel like I've betrayed you. I was attracted to her, especially when I thought she was into me. We ended up in my room and..."

"Stop being stupid, Mark. That woman is truly a certified nut-job. Look where she ended up, trying to count the pencils in a box of crayons."

"Chao, do you think I'm over the hill?"

"No. I didn't say that. I said that woman was looking for a meal ticket...not someone to be a permanent bunkmate."

"But I..."

"But what? You were attracted to her? I get it. I didn't marry a eunuch for Christ's sake. I married a man, a man with a full set of working parts."

"So..."

"So listen to me. You can look and dream with that *little brain* of yours all you want. But if I catch you touching another woman I'll take a dull knife and turn you into a female sundae."

"Chao, what the hell is a female sundae?"

"The kind with no nuts."

"Jeez, Chao. That's pretty harsh. I'll admit that I had too much alcohol and that I got out of control in Eureka. But I love you and I'm sorry. Are we ok? Should we go sit in the garden and talk?"

"Mark, I love you too. And yes, we're ok. I think it's a little too chilly to be out in the garden tonight. Cory's doing his homework, calculus I think. That'll keep him busy for at least a half hour..."

His phone rang but this time Johnson let it go to voice mail. "Hello. Detective, Johnson? This is Doctor Follers, at the Parnassus Medical Center. It's about Miss Chen..."